S0-BRP-672

THE PENGUIN POETS

D65

CHINESE VERSE

THE PENGUIN BOOK OF
CHINESE VERSE

*

TRANSLATED BY
ROBERT KOTEWALL AND NORMAN L. SMITH

*

Edited with an Introduction by
A. R. DAVIS

PENGUIN BOOKS
BALTIMORE · MARYLAND

Penguin Books Ltd, Harmondsworth, Middlesex
U.S.A.: Penguin Books Inc., 3300 Clipper Mill Road, Baltimore 11, Md
AUSTRALIA: Penguin Books Pty Ltd, 762 Whitehorse Road,
Mitcham, Victoria

—

First published 1962

—

—

Printed in Great Britain by
Western Printing Services Ltd Bristol
Set in Monotype Fournier

Cover pattern by Stephen Russ

CONTENTS

Titles in *guillemets* (« . . . ») indicate poems in the *yüeh-fu* or *tz'ŭ* song-forms, the latter being indicated by the addition of the word 'To' (see pp. 6 and 33).

ABBREVIATIONS

SPTK   *Ssŭ-pu ts'ung-k'an* editions
SPPY   *Ssŭ-pu pei-yao* editions
BSS   *Basic Sinological Series*
CTS   *Ch'üan T'ang-shih;* references to 1960 reprint in twelve volumes

period and lost his life in the succession struggle known as the 'Revolt of the Eight Princes'. Though he enjoyed a contemporary reputation rather as a scholar and writer of *fu*, he also wrote *shih* poems of quality, some thirty of which have survived.

T'AO YÜAN-MING (T'AO CH'IEN) (365–427). T'ao later came to be regarded as the greatest poet of the period between Han and T'ang (third to sixth centuries), and the greatest of all Chinese 'recluse poets'. Becoming a legend almost in his own lifetime, as a person and poet, he attracted the sympathy of numerous later poets, major and minor, who offered him their homage of imitation. In popular imagination T'ao no sooner entered political life but he left it. He was in fact involved in the sordid power-struggle of his time for more than ten years. The true interest of T'ao's personality is in the continuing conflict between his sense of duty and his inclination to reject the world and follow his own nature.

LU K'AI (*fl.* first half of fifth century). Nothing appears to be known about this Lu K'ai (not to be confused with the man of the same name who served the Northern Wei dynasty during the later part of the fifth century) beyond what can be gathered from this poem: that he was a friend of the famous historian Fan Yeh (398–445).

WANG JUNG (468–94). Native of Lin-i, Lang-yeh (near modern Nanking). A member of an important family, Wang, like so many other literary men of the Six Dynasties period (fourth to sixth centuries), was deeply involved in political intrigue, and, like many others, lost his life in consequence. In his short life he established a considerable literary reputation and was one of the most important of the Yung-ming period (483–93) poets.

FAN YÜN (451–503). Another member of the Yung-ming group of poets. Fan had a more successful and safer political career than some of his contemporaries.

T'AO HUNG-CHING (452–536), native of Mo-ling (modern Chiang-ning, Kiangsu). T'ao is best known as a Taoist writer. He spent the later half of his life as a recluse at Chü-ch'ü shan (now called Mao-shan, south-east of Chü-jung, Kiangsu). The Emperor Wu of Liang (reigned 502–49) consulted him on many matters; thus he earned the name of 'Chief minister in the Mountains'. Only six poems by T'ao have been preserved but they are all of quality.

EMPEROR YANG OF SUI (YANG KUANG) (580–618). Second Emperor of the Sui dynasty (which reunited North and South China in 589), reigned 605–16. History records the patricidal Emperor Yang as a megalomaniac and vicious character. He was, at the same time, an accomplished poet, as his surviving work demonstrates.

THE LADY HOU (*fl.* early seventh century). A concubine of the Sui Emperor Yang. According to a work of fiction *Mi-lou chi* 'the Story of the Maze Palace' (supposed to date from the ninth century but possibly later), the Lady Hou hanged herself because she was disappointed of receiving imperial favour. On her back was a bag containing her writings which were presented to the Emperor. He was deeply moved by her poems and had her buried with lavish ritual.

CONTENTS

CONTENTS

CHANG CHIU-LING (673–740). Native of Ch'ü-chiang, Kwangtung. Chang was one of the important statesmen of the earlier part of the reign of the Emperor Hsüan-tsung (713–56). In 736 he became Chief Minister, but was forced from his position by the opposition of Li Lin-fu, who made himself virtual dictator (737–52). His poetry, which brings him near the highest rank of T'ang poets, in general reflects the straightforward character of the man.

WANG WEI (701–61). Native of Ho-tung (modern Yung-chi, Shansi), painter and poet. Wang, after passing the *chin-shih* examination in 721, had a generally successful official career. He had risen to be a Grand Secretary in the Imperial Chancellery by the time of the rebellion of An Lu-shan. He fell into the hands of the rebels (756) and was forced to serve them. After the suppression of the rebellion (757) he was imprisoned but pardoned and restored to office a year later. Wang was a sincere Buddhist and, like other Chinese Buddhist writers, had a strong feeling for landscape. In the history of painting he is regarded as the founder of the Southern school of landscape painting. There was a close link between his painting and his nature poetry which prompted Su Shih's famous remark 'In his poetry there is painting, in his painting, poetry.' Wang was a very great master of the *chüeh-chü* ('cut-short') quatrain.

LI PO (701–62). He and his contemporary Tu Fu are regarded as the two greatest poets of the greatest period of *shih* poetry. Li left his home at Ch'ang-ming, Szechwan, about 720, and for twenty years wandered from place to place, occasionally seeking official employment but not through the examinations. For a short period (742–4) he enjoyed favour as a court poet at the capital Ch'ang-an, but thereafter he resumed his wanderings. Late in his life he was involved in the revolt of Prince Lin and banished (758) to Yeh-lang (Yunnan), but pardoned before he reached there. A great drinker and dabbler in Taoism, Li is the supreme example of irresponsibility among Chinese poets.

TU FU (712–70). Tu Fu, unlike Li Po, got an official post fairly late in life (758), when the normal examination system had temporarily broken down during the rebellion of An Lu-shan. He met Li Po in 745, and was deeply impressed by the older poet in spite of, or perhaps because of, their very different personalities. He continued to write poems to, or about, Li for many years after. Tu was essentially serious, and his work, in contrast to Li Po's, commonly shows a greater interest in the condition of his times (he experienced great personal distress at the time of the rebellion). His emotional range seems greater than Li's and he is also a more intellectual poet. Of the two his immediate influence was greater.

TS'ÊN SHÊN (715–70). After passing the *chin-shih* examination in 744, he served for some ten years in the north-west frontier areas (corresponding to the modern provinces of Sinkiang, Kansu, and Shensi). This long experience in remote, physically harsh areas, where there was constant fighting, gave much of his poetry a subject matter not very commonly seen in T'ang poetry apart from the works of his contemporary Kao Shih (? 700–65) who saw similar service.

CONTENTS

CONTENTS

CHANG CHI (c. 768–830). Was the closest friend and adherent of Han Yü, who, in his turn, greatly admired Chang's work. His whole life seems to have been spent in poverty and he was early afflicted with weak eye-sight. His great concern was with social injustice, which concern he expressed in *yüeh-fu* songs. Po Chü-i, another friend, wrote his political songs under Chang's influence.

YANG CHÜ-YÜAN (c. 760–832). Native of P'u-chou (modern Yung-chi, Shansi). Yang followed a normal official career after passing the *chin-shih* examination in 789, but did not rise very high. He was an older friend of Po Chü-i and Yüan Chên and gave Yüan his first lessons in poetry.

PO CHÜ-I (772–846). Native of Hsia-kuei (north-east of modern Wei-nan, Shensi), Po enjoyed a moderately successful official career in the capital and in provincial posts. He was Governor first of Hangchow and then of Soochow between the years 822 and 826. He spent his last years in the eastern capital Lo-yang, where he held his last public post (831–3). He was the author of two of the longest and most popular poems of the T'ang period, *Ch'ang-hên ko* ('Song of everlasting remorse', which tells the story of the Emperor Hsüan-tsung and his concubine Yang Kuei-fei), and the *P'i-p'a hsing* ('Lute song'). Besides these narrative works, Po also wrote 'new *yüeh-fu*' under the influence of his friend Chang Chi, which are attempts at social criticism, but the great bulk of his collection is occasional verse. He aimed at a general simplicity of expression which partly accounts for his immense contemporary popularity and for his popularity in Japan. In modern China he has been one of the most studied T'ang poets.

xiii

YÜAN CHÊN (779–831). Was a descendant of the Northern Wei (Tartar) imperial family (ruling in north China fifth to sixth centuries). His thirty-year friendship with Po Chü-i was probably the most celebrated literary friendship in Chinese history. Though possessing greater administrative capacity than Po, he lacked political success. He became Chief Minister for a short period in 822, but most of his career was passed away from the capital. Yüan and Po were seldom able to meet but exchanged letters and poems continually.

CHIA TAO (779–843). Originally a Buddhist monk, returned to secular life at the urging of Han Yü, who persuaded him to go in for the *chin-shih* examination. Chia repeatedly failed. His circumstances were hard, like those of Mêng Chiao with whom he is generally coupled, and his distress constantly appears in his poetry. Chia, from various anecdotes and from his own account, appears as a laborious seeker after the telling line.

P'EI I-CHIH (*fl.* first half of the ninth century, *chin-shih* 815). P'ei probably belonged to the important P'ei family of Wên-hsi, Shansi, which produced two Chief Ministers during the first half of the ninth century. He became a Vice-president of the Grand Secretariat during the reign of the Emperor Wên-tsung (827–40) but later served in provincial appointments. The *Complete T'ang Poems* contains fifty-seven poems by P'ei.

CHU CH'ING-YÜ (*fl.* first half of ninth century: *chin-shih* 826). Native of Yüeh-chou (modern Shao-hsing, Chekiang), a follower of Chang Chi.

TU CH'IU (TU CH'IU-NIANG; first half of ninth century). What is known of Tu Ch'iu, authoress of *Gold thread coat*, comes from Tu Mu's preface to his poem *Tu Ch'iu-niang*. According to this, she was first a concubine of Li Ch'i, but after the latter's revolt and death she was sent to the imperial harem. Later she was allowed to return to her native place, Chin-ling (modern Nanking). Tu Mu wrote his poem to her when 'passing through Chin-ling and being moved by her poverty and old age'.

TU MU (803–52). Had a normal and fairly successful official career; he achieved in his last years a high post in the Grand Secretariat. His poetry bridges the transition from 'Mid T'ang' to 'Late T'ang'. 'Little Tu', as he was called to distinguish him from the great Tu Fu, shows sometimes the quality of greatness, as in the magnificent description in *Travelling in the Mountains*.

WÊN T'ING-YÜN (812–70). Native of T'ai-yüan, Shansi. Wên's name is joined with that of Li Shang-yin to typify the 'Late T'ang' style of elegant and erudite poetry. It is a commonplace of old Chinese criticism that Wên 'had talent but lacked conduct', that is he was a frivolous, pleasure-loving person. It was his association with singing-girls that helped to make him the first great writer of the *tz'ŭ* lyric and the founder of the tenth-century 'Hua-chien' school of *tz'ŭ* poetry.

LI SHANG-YIN (813–58). The most important of the 'Late T'ang' poets, he had a relatively undistinguished official career, though at different times he formed connexions with both the main political cliques of his day. His contemporary literary reputation was considerable and he exerted an influence upon the poetry of the next hundred years and more, turning it into the path of allusiveness and the search for elegant, often obscure expression. His love poems are his particular contribution to Chinese poetry.

HSÜ HUN (*fl.* first half of ninth century, *chin-shih* 832). Made his home at Tan-yang, Kiangsu. Hsü was a descendant of Hsü Yü-shih, who had been a Chief Minister under the Emperor Kao-tsung in the early T'ang period, and he himself had a moderately distinguished official career. His work is stylistically similar to that of Li Shang-yin and Wên T'ing-yün.

YEN YÜN (*fl.* first half of ninth century). Native of Wu-hsing, Chekiang. Only this one poem by Yen has been preserved and little is known of him save that he was an acquaintance of Tu Mu.

CHAO KU (ninth century, *chin-shih* 842). Native of Shan-yang (modern Huai-an, Kiangsu). Chao was a contemporary of Tu Mu, who admired his poetry.

SHÊN HSÜN (ninth century, *chin-shih* in the period 841–6). Native of Wu-hsien, Kiangsu. Shên was murdered together with his wife by a slave, which gives a rather suspicious appropriateness to this poem, the only poem ascribed to Shên in the *Complete T'ang Poems*.

CONTENTS

CONTENTS

CONTENTS

CONTENTS

WANG YÜ-CH'ÊNG (954–1001). Native of Chü-yeh, Shantung. Wang, who took Tu Fu and Po Chü-i as his models, was one of the first poets to react against the *Hsi-k'un* style dominant at the beginning of the Sung period. The poem *Written at Ch'i-an commandery* does not appear in his collected works *Hsiao-ch'u chi*.

FAN CHUNG-YEN (989–1052). Native of Wu-hsien, Kiangsu, a Confucian reformer, was one of the most important political figures of the third and fourth decades of the eleventh century, becoming a Grand Councillor in 1043. He also spent several years in frontier commands. He left much *shih*-poetry but it is his *tz'ŭ* of which only six specimens have survived that are especially admired by Chinese literary historians.

OU-YANG HSIU (1007–72). Native of Lu-ling, Kiangsi, was the acknowledged leader of the literary world of his generation and a major political figure. Like his friend Fan Chung-yen, he believed strongly in the practical application of Confucianism to politics. It was Ou-yang's position of influence, and the example of his own writing that largely contributed to the success of the *ku-wên* prose movement begun by Han Yü in the T'ang period. In his *shih*-poetry, as in his prose, he shows a directness and simplicity combined with great fluency. His *tz'ŭ*, which some have held to be falsely attributed to him, because they believed this great Confucian master would not have stooped to writing love poetry, still remain close to the Five Dynasties style, particularly to that of Fêng Yen-chi.

CONTENTS

WANG AN-SHIH (1021–86). Native of Lin-ch'uan, Kiangsi, Wang became in his own lifetime, and has since remained, a very controversial figure on account of his extensive reform programme, carried through between 1069 and 1074. Though some critics have extended their dislike of his political actions to his literary works, his achievements as a prose writer and poet cannot justly be denied. His *chüeh-chü* ('cut-short') poems have been greatly admired.

LIU YUNG (first half of eleventh century, *chin-shih* 1034). May be regarded as the most influential representative of the new direction in early Sung *tz̆'ŭ* writing towards longer forms, more colloquial diction and more detailed description.

SU SHIH (1036–1101). Native of Mei-shan, Szechwan. Su was an opponent of Wang An-shih's reform policy, and his political career followed the alternation of periods of office in the capital and relegation to provincial appointments of the conservative party. Thus, after Wang's rise to power, Su had a long period in the provinces from 1071 to 1084. After a return to the capital (1085) he went as governor to Hangchow (1089–91), and after a further brief return to the capital, was banished to Hui-chou, Kwangtung (1094) and then to Hainan island (1097). Su was not only one of China's greatest writers, outstanding in both verse and prose, but a great calligrapher and painter. His immediate family was one of the most remarkable in the history of literature, since his father Su Hsün and his younger brother

Su Chê also rank as major writers. He felt a strong affinity with T'ao Yuan-ming and wrote poems to 'harmonize' with all the earlier poet's work, but Su probably had the more genial personality. He used the *tz'ŭ* form widely for all types of subject and thus increased its range.

YEN CHI-TAO (*fl.* second half of eleventh century), son of Yen Shu (991–1055) who was himself one of the best known *tz'ŭ* writers of the early Sung period. In contrast to his father, Chi-tao seems to have been an arrogant, difficult person, and through failure in public life he was reduced to poverty. Many of his *tz'ŭ*, while possessing his father's elegant phrasing, have a bitter nostalgic expression.

CHOU PANG-YEN (1057–1121). Native of Ch'ien-t'ang (modern Hangchow), gained entry into official life by the presentation of a very long descriptive *fu* on the Northern Sung capital. He held a number of appointments in the capital of the kind usual for those with a literary reputation. As a skilled musician, coming at the end of a period of rapid development in *tz'ŭ* writing, he contributed greatly to the technical perfection and formal standardization of this many-patterned type of poetry. His *tz'ŭ* thus became very influential models.

CONTENTS

group. (Lü did not include himself but later critics did so.)
Twenty-six of his *tz̆'ŭ* poems have survived.

LU YU (1125–1210). Native of Shan-yin (modern Shaohsing,
Chekiang), is generally regarded as the greatest of the Southern
Sung poets. He is said at first to have been kept out of official
life by the jealousy of the Chief Minister Ch'in Kuei. Later, for
some time, he enjoyed the favour of the Emperor Hsiao-tsung
(1163–80) but was afterwards banished to the provinces. In
middle age he saw service in Szechwan, for part of the time on
the staff of Fan Ch'êng-ta. His early masters were poets of the
Kiangsi school but Lu cannot properly be included in this
school. Although he produced an immense amount of nature-
poetry (he ranks as China's most prolific poet), the keynote of
his writing is his intense patriotism, his desire for the recovery
of the lost north.

FAN CH'ÊNG-TA (1126–93). Native of Wu-hsien, Kiangsu,
had an important and successful public career. He was entrusted
with an embassy to the Chin ruler of North China in 1164 and
later did valuable service in checking the attacks of the T'u-fan
(Tibetan) tribes, while military governor in Szechwan. Beside
his poetry, his surviving writings include journals, a local
history of his native place, and a work on chrysanthemums.
As a *shih* poet he was grouped in the Kiangsi school of pastoral
poets, and he treated generally similar themes in his *tz̆'ŭ*.

HSIN CH'I-CHI (1140–1207). Native of Li-ch'êng, Shantung.
As a young man (1161) Hsin served with Kêng Ching who
raised a revolt in Shantung against the Chin Tartars, who had
conquered North China. The revolt failed, but through it
Hsin came to the notice of the Southern Sung government and
embarked on a long career of civil and military appointments.

His intense patriotism has won him great popularity in recent times. Earlier critics found a roughness of diction and style in his *tz̒ŭ*, but their strong and virile character is a virtue in modern eyes. Though the current attention to Hsin may be somewhat exaggerated, it is not wholly misplaced.

CHU SHU-CHÊN probably flourished about the end of the twelfth and the beginning of the thirteenth century. Very little is known of her antecedents or her life, but a greater number of her *shih* and *tz̒ŭ* poems have been preserved than of any other woman writer of her time or of any earlier period. An unhappy marriage is believed to have been the inspiration of much of her poetry.

CHIAO-JU-HUI (date uncertain: eleventh to twelfth century). A Buddhist monk.

TAI FU-KU was born in 1167: the date of his death is not known, but he lived to be more than eighty. He was one of the better poets among the Chiang-hu group which arose at the end of the Southern Sung period in opposition to the Kiangsi school, which had been dominant throughout the period.

CHANG LIANG-CH̒ÊN (twelfth century, *chin-shih* 1163). Minor member of the Chiang-hu group.

CONTENTS

CONTENTS

minister Yen Sung who had him imprisoned and executed. This poem is said to have been composed and recited by him on his way to execution.

LI P'AN-LUNG (1524–70). Native of Li-ch'êng, Shantung. Li, in his official career (he passed the *chin-shih* examination in 1544), rose to the position of a provincial judge. As a poet he was named one of the 'Seven Masters of the Chia-ching period' (1522–66).

KUEI TZŬ-MOU (1563–1606). Native of Kun-shan, Kiangsu, was the youngest son of Kuei Yu-kuang (1506–71) the most famous Ming prose-writer.

HUANG YU-TSAO (sixteenth century). Woman poet.

HSÜ T'UNG (sixteenth century: *chü-jên* (provincial graduate) 1588). Native of Min-hsien (modern Min-hou, Fukien).

CH'I CHING-YÜN (sixteenth to early seventeenth century). A singing girl.

SHIH JUN-CHANG (1619–83). Native of Hsüan-ch'êng, Anhui. Shih had a successful and honoured career and enjoyed

distinguished official career. He was at the same time one of the major critics and theorists of his period. He gave importance to musical effect and to suggestion rather than direct statement. His extreme use of classical allusions turned much of his poetry into complicated puzzles which do not find favour with modern critics.

HSIAO-CH'ING (FÊNG YÜAN-YÜAN; mid-seventeenth century). Is said to have become the concubine of a man of Hangchow with the same surname, Fêng, and to have died of grief in her eighteenth year, because his wife would not tolerate her.

WANG CHI-WU (1645–1725). Native of T'ai-ts'ang, Kiangsu, achieved the position of Prefect of Shaohsing, Chekiang.

HSÜ LAN (late seventeenth to early eighteenth century). Native of Ch'ang-shu, Kiangsu. Student of Wang Shih-chên, Hsü was noted for his unusual diction; in this he was compared with the T'ang poet Li Ho (791–817).

WAN PANG-JUNG (eighteenth century: *chü-jên* (provincial graduate) 1720). Native of Hsiang-ch'êng, Honan. Wan was one of the 184 candidates recommended for the special metropolitan examination in 1736 but was unsuccessful. Later he became magistrate of Hsin-hsien, Shantung.

YÜAN MEI (1716–98). Native of Ch'ien-t'ang (Hangchow), Yüan began writing at an early age and was the youngest candidate for the special metropolitan examination of 1736; he did not pass. However, he obtained the *chin-shih* degree in 1739 and became a scholar in the Hanlin Academy. From 1742 to 1748 he was magistrate of a number of places in Kiangsu but thereafter retired from official life, living by his writings at his famous villa, Sui-yüan. Openly avowing that the object of life is enjoyment, he rejected many traditional attitudes. He became notorious (later famous) for his encouragement of his women-pupils whose poetry he published. In spite of his unconventionality, he numbered many leading political and literary figures, often of opposed views, among his friends, and his contemporary popularity was very great. In poetry and poetry criticism he stood for freedom and individuality: he seems to have been far more interested in the poetry of his own period than in the great poets of the past.

CHAO KUAN-HSIAO (eighteenth century). Native of Kuei-an, Chekiang.

CONTENTS

of important diplomatic and consular appointments in Japan (1877–82), the U.S.A. (1882–5), London (1890–1), and Singapore (1891–4). After his recall to China he was prominent in the reform movement which culminated in the Hundred Days Reform of 1898. Huang was appointed minister to Japan at that time, but, with the suppression of the reformers by the Empress Dowager, never went to his post. For the last years of his life he lived in retirement at Chia-ying. In his poetry, as in his political ideas, he was considerably influenced by his foreign experiences, but he did not abandon traditional forms in spite of his professed desire to do so.

LIU TA-PAI (1880–1932). Native of Shao-hsing, Chekiang, poet and literary critic. A *chü-jên* (provincial graduate) under the Ch'ing dynasty, Liu held a series of educational posts under the republic. He was among the first to attempt vernacular poetry after the Literary Revolution.

HU SHIH (b. 1891). Studied English literature, philosophy, and political science at Cornell, and wrote a doctoral thesis at Colombia (1915–17). While he was in America, he formed his ideas of a literary revolution to which he gave expression in *Hsin Ch'ing-nien* (*La Jeunesse*), a periodical edited by Ch'ên Tu-hsiu. The movement led by Hu Shih and Ch'ên Tu-hsiu had an almost immediate success. Hu's main contribution to the movement was through his literary and philosophical studies, rather than through creative writing. He did, however, write the first new poetry, which has thus a historical interest. From 1917 to 1926 he was a professor at Peking National University, the stronghold of the literary revolutionaries, and returned there in 1931. During the war with Japan he was Chinese ambassador to the U.S.A. After the war he returned again to Peking National University as Chancellor, leaving just before the Communist entry in 1949. As the most important figure of the Literary Revolution living outside the mainland, his ideas and writings have received endless criticism there in recent years.

CONTENTS

PING-HSIN (pseud. of HSIEH WAN-YING, b. 1902). Native of Min-hou, Fukien. She became known in the early years of the Literary Revolution, while she was still a student at Yenching University, as a writer of short stories. She has been China's most successful contemporary woman writer.

INTRODUCTION

THIS anthology was not compiled with the object of illustrating the history of poetry in China. The two translators worked together over a number of years, translating at their will until the pages grew. In the end they produced a selection of Chinese verse, ranging more widely than most which have yet appeared, over the whole period of verse-writing in China, a period of more than 2,500 years. They translated what pleased them and what seemed to go well into English, without too much regard to native Chinese views of poetic stature. To preface their selection with a historical account of Chinese poetry and poets in a strictly chronological manner would probably not introduce the reader very successfully to the translations, and the translations in their turn would not wholly illustrate the historical account. In any case no Western scholar of Chinese has as yet the resources to write an adequate historical account of Chinese verse, nor does the evidence suggest that any very complete study is likely to come at present from China itself. It would seem better, then, to try to describe some of the particular characteristics of Chinese verse, the context in which they have arisen, Chinese views of poetry, past and present, and also current attitudes to the immense heritage from former times.

Since the approach of Western students of Chinese literature has inevitably been strongly influenced by the direction taken by native scholars, a preliminary look at the situation of literature and learning in twentieth-century China will be relevant. The past fifty years have witnessed a great revolution in education and literature, which, like her political revolution, has owed much to the impact of the West. If we ignore all political considerations, we may see as a very powerful motive for this revolution, the recognition of the need of a modern society for a broadly based literacy and education. Until the present century literature, at any rate recognized literature, had been very much the province of the few, and had been written in a highly artificial language, remote from the usages of current speech. Traditional Chinese writing in the artificial literary language was indeed bound to come to an end with the fall of the type of society which sustained it. The ending did not essentially require the violent attacks which the literary reformers launched upon it – understandable as those attacks were in the immediate revolutionary situation. Their vehement political attitudes to the literature of the past have had not altogether fortunate results in the field of literary history. Although the Chinese in the past produced many works of bibliography and literary criticism, they had not before the present century attempted any general history of their literature. We have to remember that before the late nineteenth century they had little awareness of foreign literatures existing outside the Chinese cultural orbit, and the peculiar conditions of Chinese literary development had tended to mask the features of change. When the literary revolutionaries from 1917 onwards pulled down the edifice of traditional literature, there was at last no doubt that an era had ended, that literature might be surveyed historically. But the survey was usually to have particular objectives, a particular bias. To replace the former literary language, the revolutionaries turned to *pai-hua*, 'plain speech'. Writing in *pai-hua* had in fact gone on in China for a very long time, and from at least the twelfth century there is a strongly established secondary literature, not officially recognized in its own period, written in a language near to contemporary speech. This secondary literature, consisting chiefly of works of fiction and opera, had been addressed to an audience much wider than the scholar-official class for whom poetry and prose in the literary language were produced. It was primarily a literature of entertainment. In their need for models for the New Literature, and the desire for models was deeply ingrained in Chinese writers, the reformers went to *pai-hua* works of the preceding centuries. The change in the status of old *pai-hua* novels and other writings was dramatic, and the revaluation of all past literature has been drastic. Thus the compilation of general histories of literature in China was largely begun at a time when what had occupied a lower and despised position had been raised to the place of supreme importance. In the particular field of poetry the result has been that poems written during the last three dynasties (from the thirteenth to the nineteenth centuries) in the literary language, some millions in extant number, have been almost universally dismissed as imitative and worthless, and the only form of poetry from this very long period to receive much consideration is the operatic aria or the popular song. For the literary historian this kind of approach is intolerable, because literature is not simply a sociological phenomenon, nor is good literature solely a matter of language and form. The Chinese, however, have fought and continue to fight the political battles of the present backwards through the history of their past. We perhaps need always to be mindful of the inner compulsion upon those who have been forced out of their traditional course by external pressures, to reform the links of their present with their past, in the current cliché, the 'national heritage'. In People's China the important literary criteria are 'feeling for the people' and patriotism, and it is interesting to observe how many great writers of the past have gradually been discovered to possess these qualities. An interesting example is that of Li Yü, a poet represented in this anthology. With the maximum disadvantages of class-origin (he was the last ruler of the Southern T'ang dynasty in the tenth century and on evidence an ineffectual, pleasure-loving ruler), he yet received a more or less favourable verdict in his 'trial' by critics in Peking in 1956: among other pleas made for him was the one that the people (of today) liked his poems. Enough has now been said to indicate the rather partisan nature of the lead that the very small band of Western scholars is likely to receive from their present colleagues in China.

Apart from their insistence upon the importance of the popular, or at least what may be argued to have connexion with the people, in literature, modern Chinese critics tend to hold to what may be called a 'golden age' view of literary development. In any particular period some new literary form reaches its peak of development, its golden age, and thereafter must give place to *the* form of the next period. According to such a view a writer must, to achieve the name of greatness, be an exponent of the appropriate literary form of his time. The golden age of *shih*, the most characteristic form of Chinese poetry, is the T'ang dynasty (A.D. 618–907) and thus no later *shih*-poet can be allowed the same standing as a T'ang man. While this 'golden age' view is not without some foundation, it is very much an over-simplification and leads to the ignoring of vast areas of Chinese literature. For example one would not realize from many recent Chinese works that the prose-poem form called *fu*, which had its golden age in the second and first centuries B.C., continued to be used extensively until recent times. In general, literary forms, once created, tended to persist up to the great divide of this century. If the historical study of Chinese literature is to progress, a less narrow selection of material will need to be made. Also there is a clear need to move away from the present over-emphasis upon form.

The most important characteristic of Chinese poetry from the point of view of its appeal to the Western reader is its intimate expression of personal feeling. To put it in other words, it is the presence of that quality which enables us to know the man through his work without any other biographical matter. The reader will recognize the complete achievement of this quality in the two poems by T'ao Yüan-ming (A.D. 365–427) presented in this anthology. T'ao is the first truly great writer of personal poetry in China, and it is possible to take him as a point of perfection up to which to trace the process of its attainment.

In the sixteenth-century anthology *Ku-shih-chi* by Fêng Wei-no, and other similar anthologies, one may find collected some number of songs which purport to come from the high antiquity of the third and second millennia B.C. Now that the traditional history of these remote periods has been reduced to a more appropriate status of myth and legend, all these songs have had to be rejected as 'fake antiques', though the time of their invention was often as long ago as the later part of the first millennium B.C. The oldest Chinese poetry known to us is that contained in the anthology called first in Chinese *Shih* (i.e. the same word as that later used generically for the main form of poetry), and later, when it became one of the chief Confucian scriptures, *Shih-ching* (*ching* = canon). This *Songs* (or later *Book of Songs*) would seem to have existed as a collection, very much in its transmitted form, by the time of Confucius (551–479 B.C.). Later Confucian tradition made the Master himself the editor of the *Songs*, selecting the present 300 odd from an original 3,000, but only ultra-conservatives still accept this. How this collection came to form an entity is indeed not known, nor can we say with any certainty the range of time which it represents. Old ascriptions of some of its pieces to the beginning of the Chou period in the eleventh century B.C. remain doubtful. Only a few of the songs can be given precise and secure dates. In the absence of reliable dating for the majority of the songs, the attempt to see a pattern of development within the anthology, and thus in the earliest Chinese poetry, can only be speculative. This collection contains both religious and secular songs: some composed for the entertainment of the rulers and feudal nobles, and some of popular origin. The songs of one of the three major divisions of the book, the *Kuo-fêng* section ('The Airs of the States') were later, in works of the Confucian school, stated to have been collected from various states by officers of the Chou kings to whom the states owed allegiance that the kings 'might observe the manners of the people'. Modern linguistic study upon the *Shih* does not seem to confirm this: the songs exhibit a general homogeneity of language. It is of course possible that they have undergone adaptation at the hands of court musicians. Among the themes of the whole collection are to be found courtship and marriage, agriculture and war, hunting and feasting, praise of ancestors, eulogy of great men. Whether sad or gay in tone, these songs are expressions of common or collective emotions; they are still far from personal poetry. Among them are very many pieces excellent of their kind.

It is probably true to say that it is only very recently, almost for the first time since the period in which they were composed, that these songs have been appreciated simply for their poetic quality. For Confucius and the Confucian school the book became a manual for didactic exposition not of literature but of ethics and politics. The feudal society depicted in the *Songs* was beginning to break up by the sixth century B.C. The power of the Chou kings over their feudatories had already begun to decline in the eighth century B.C., when their capital had to be moved eastwards under 'barbarian' pressure. The feudal states were growing fewer in number, but larger and more powerful. Material progress as China moved out of the bronze into the iron age, the improvement of agriculture, the development of commerce, and an increased social mobility are characteristic of the later centuries of the Chou period. China was struggling through the time of the Warring States (fifth to third centuries B.C.) towards its first united centralized empire, and a new order of society. With the Chou kings relegated to a position of complete political impotence, the issue was fought to decide which of a small number of great states was to found the new empire. The sixth to the third centuries B.C. were a dynamic period in Chinese history, one which is generally regarded as the most creative in Chinese philosophy: the period of the 'Hundred Schools', whose exponents contended as fiercely with words as the political leaders (whose favour they sought to attract) with troops. The contribution of this period to Chinese literature, apart from its particular achievements among its philosophical writings, was a great advance in the range and flexibility of language. Naturally the development of language and philosophy went hand in hand: thinking promoted language and language promoted thought.

In the midst of this political and social thought we find some expression of views upon the use of literature, but it is upon the use of already existing literature, in particular the *Songs*, not upon the creation of new literature. The Confucian attitude may be illustrated by the saying in the *Analects*:

> My disciples, why do none of you study the *Songs*? By the *Songs* one may be stimulated, one may observe, one may be sociable, one may express resentment. One may make a near use of them in the service of one's father, a distant use in the service of one's ruler. From them one may have much knowledge of the names of birds, beasts, and plants.
>
> (Book XVII, 9)

The *Songs* were to have a social, political, and educational force. We see here the beginnings of the idea of the social utility of literature, which exerted very great pressure upon Chinese writers throughout history and is still potent under a new name. The chief opponents of the Confucians in the third century B.C., the Taoists and the Legalists whom the Taoists greatly influenced, had no such use for literature. For the Taoists, culture and learning obstructed the attainment of natural simplicity; for the Legalists, the *Songs* were one of the 'lice' which diverted the people of the state from the only essential tasks of agriculture and war. The western state of Ch'in, which finally overcame its rivals and established its short-lived dynasty in 221 B.C., adopted the Legalist doctrines and attempted the suppression of the *Shih* in the famous 'Burning of the Books' which is dated 213 B.C. But under the Han, which, succeeding Ch'in in 206 B.C., and building upon its foundation, made firm the pattern of Chinese political organization that lasted until modern times, the Confucians gradually won state acceptance of their doctrines and the elevation of their texts, among them the *Shih*, into the position of scriptures. From the Han period onwards the *Shih-ching* accumulated a great mass of scholastic interpretation: its love-songs became an allegory of the relations between ruler and minister.

The later centuries of the Chou period produced no second 'Book of Songs', Pan Ku (A.D. 32–92) wrote in c. 30 of his *History of the Former Han Dynasty*:

After the Spring and Autumn period (722–481 B.C.) the way of Chou gradually declined, and embassies seeking songs were not sent to the various states. The scholars who studied the *Songs* went into retirement and lived among the common people. Then arose the *fu* of worthy men disappointed of their ambitions.

This *fu* in fact became *the* literary form of the Han period. The Chinese have never regarded the *fu* as pure poetry, even when, as commonly, it is completely rhymed and has a regular metre – or perhaps it is more true to say that the Chinese categories *wên* and *shih* do not exactly correspond to our ideas of prose and verse. The term *shih*, first used for the *Songs*, was always kept for verse forms which were singable or felt to be close to song. The *fu* was classified as *wên*, which we call, in opposition to *shih*, 'prose', but we should add the qualification that Chinese prose was often influenced by verse rhythms: the *fu* contributed much to the development of the highly rhythmical 'parallel prose'. The *fu*, as is stated in the chapter of the *History of the Former Han Dynasty* just quoted, was not sung.

As an example of a 'worthy man disappointed of his ambitions', Pan Ku cites the minister of Ch'u, Ch'ü Yüan, who 'encountering slander and grieving for his country, wrote *fu* to express criticism'. From the Han period on, Ch'ü Yüan was believed to have been a loyal minister of King Huai of Ch'u (reigned 328–299 B.C.), who through slander lost his ruler's favour, and was later banished, eventually drowning himself in

the river Mi-lo. He became, during the Han period and there-
after throughout history, a heroic figure with whom the Chinese
scholar-official, disappointed of public recognition, sought to
identify himself. In People's China a particular emphasis has
been set upon his patriotism, and he has displaced Confucius as
the great figure of antiquity.

The *fu* to which Pan Ku must specifically refer is the 373-
lines-long *Li-sao* (*Encountering Sorrow*). Pan Ku, as a Confu-
cian, readily believed that the *Li-sao* had been written by Ch'ü
Yüan as a deliberate political allegory, and Wang I, the second-
century commentator of the anthology *Ch'u-tz'ü* (literally
'Words of Ch'u') in which the *Li-sao* appears, interprets the
allegory. Had the *Li-sao* alone survived, its acceptance as a
political allegory, curious though its expression still would seem,
would perhaps not be too difficult. However, along with the *Li-
sao*, the *Ch'u-tz'ü* anthology contains a number of other pieces,
also ascribed to Ch'ü Yüan. It is the relation between these other
pieces and the *Li-sao* that the huge and ever-growing volume of
Ch'u-tz'ü studies has yet failed completely satisfactorily to
explain. For some of these other pieces, for example the series
entitled *Chiu-ko* (*The Nine Songs*), are undoubtedly connected
with religious practices of the state of Ch'u, which was centred
in the Yangtse valley and thus had been only on the extreme
fringe of the Yellow River valley civilization of early China: in
the later part of the Chou period it had become one of the chief
contestants for supreme power. *The Nine Songs* represent a kind
of dramatic performance in which a divine love-affair is por-
trayed. To reconstruct either its technique or indeed its purposes,
we are forced upon speculation, scattered references to *shamans*
or spirit invokers throughout Chinese literature, and comparison
with other cultures. It is presumed that the gods or goddesses
whose names give titles to the separate songs in this series were
invoked by female or male *shamans* in the manner of courtship,
with the object of securing their blessings. The commentator

Wang I affirmed that Ch'ü Yüan had composed these songs,
after observing the religious rites and song-and-dance music of
the people: he implies that Ch'ü Yüan was providing an elegant
version of these religious songs, while, at the same time, express-
ing his own grief and, in an allegorical manner, his censure of
his ruler. This suggestion seems quite untenable, and its un-
tenability must in turn raise doubts upon the *Li-sao*'s being
simply a political allegory. For the *Li-sao* uses the same language
of love, the symbolism of flowers and journeys through the air
with god-like appointments, which appear in the *Nine Songs*.
The *Ch'u-tz'ŭ* poems are not suitable for inclusion in a general
anthology of Chinese verse, since they would require to be
accompanied by considerable discussion: thus no example is
given here. They cannot be translated in many cases without a
satisfying theory of their overall intention. I have devoted some
space to mention of them, both because of their intrinsic import-
ance in the history of Chinese poetry, and also because the little
I have said may serve to emphasize the Confucian insistence
upon social criticism as a function of poetry. Many Chinese
poets of various periods did attempt such criticism by allegory
and allusion; many Chinese critics too have discovered political
reference where almost certainly it was not intended. A part of
the *Li-sao*, as it has come down to us, may well have a critical
intention, but it seems highly improbable that this is the purpose
of the whole.

The early *Ch'u-tz'ŭ* poems may be regarded as the immediate
ancestors of the Han *fu*. Both show in increasing degree a sen-
suous delight in the use of words. Clearly the consciousness of
the art of literature was growing, and exuberant experimentation
with language is readily explicable. The *fu* of the Former Han
period (second and first centuries B.C.) was very much a public
art. It was written in and for the courts of the Emperor and the
imperial princes. We may say that where the thinkers of the
Warring States had offered philosophical arguments to rulers,

the writers of Han now offered literature. The Han *fu* are so obviously a product of court life and have so little connexion with 'the people' that current Chinese literary histories are inclined to damn them with the word 'euphuistic' and rather to underestimate their contribution to literature. I should like to quote here a *fu* of the Later Han period, which may illustrate very significant progress towards the personal poetry that reached perfection with T'ao Yüan-ming. Chang Hêng (A.D. 78–139) famous as an astronomer and mathematician, had written what would be regarded as more typical *fu* on the life of the Han capital cities, as well as this *Return to the Country*.[1]

> I have spent in the city an eternity of time,
> Without clear plan to aid the age.
> Vainly looking on the stream to admire the fish,
> And waiting for the River to run clear, with no time fixed.
> I am moved by the great-heartedness of Master Ts'ai,
> Who followed after Master T'ang to obtain removal of his
> doubts.[2]
> Truly the way of Heaven is subtle and obscure:
> So I shall follow the Fisherman[3] and share his joy.
> Striding over the dust and going far away,
> From the world I shall take a long farewell.
>
> So then in Mid-Spring's fair month,
> When the season is mild, the air clear,
> When plains and marshes are luxuriant,
> With every flower in blossom,
> When the fish-hawk beats his wings,
> And the oriole plaintively sings,

1. *Wên-hsüan* (SPTK) *c.* 15, 25b. I thank the Australian National University for permission to reprint this translation of mine from the Twentieth George Ernest Morrison Lecture in Ethnology.
2. Ts'ai Tsê (third century B.C.), who had unsuccessfully sought office from a number of rulers, consulted the physiognomist T'ang Chü and was told that he would live for another forty-three years. He later became chief minister in Ch'in. 3. A typical recluse.

Side by side, they fly up and down,
Kuan-kuan, they cry to one another,
Among them I shall wander
And so delight my feelings.

Then when the dragon cries in the great marsh,
And the tiger roars among the hills,
Above I shall let fly the slender string,[1]
Below I shall angle in the long-flowing waters.
Striking against the arrow, the bird will die;
Covetous of the bait, the fish will swallow the hook.
So I shall pull down the bird that soared free among the clouds
And have hanging on my line the sand-fish that hid in the depths.

Then when the bright spirit[2] suddenly declines,
And Wang-shu[3] takes his place,
Enjoying to the full the perfect pleasure of wandering about,
Although it is evening, I shall forget my weariness.
Moved by the warning left for us by Master Lao,[4]
I shall turn back my carriage to my rustic hut.
I shall pluck beautiful tunes from the five-string lute,
And recite the works of the Duke of Chou and of Confucius,
Plying my brush and ink, I shall start to compose,
And set forth the model ways of the Three Emperors.
Since I give my heart rein beyond worldly limits,
What shall I know of glory and disgrace?

That Chang Hêng could contemplate a rural existence in which he could devote himself to leisurely pleasures and literary pursuits has important social and economic implications. In fact, with the development of large-scale private ownership of land, the official class which provided the many functionaries, central

1. An arrow with a string attached for bringing down birds.
2. The sun.
3. The charioteer of the moon.
4. 'Galloping and hunting make a man's mind go mad' (*Lao-tzŭ c.* 12).

1

and local, that the bureaucratically organized Han empire required, had established a strong economic base. It had thus become possible for a man like Chang Hêng, who was dissatisfied with his advancement at the capital, to retire to the family estate. The official-gentry class, thrown up by the development of Han society, became a permanent feature of the Chinese social structure. Men of this class were to be the possessors of learning and the makers of literature. For under the Han also the principle that the administrators of the Empire should be educated men had been established. They were to be educated in the Confucian orthodoxy which the Han Confucians had created out of the simple sayings of Confucius, modified by the teachings of the Confucian and other schools to suit the needs of the Han state. This orthodoxy was disseminated through the imperial university, opened in 124 B.C., which is known during the Later Han period to have had more than 30,000 students on its enrolment. Under the Han, thus took place the beginnings of the state education and state examination system which were a vital support for the maintenance of the position of the scholar-official class.

A little closer attention must now be given to poetic form. In all traditional Chinese poetry the metrical unit is the word not the syllable as in European verse. Particular Chinese metres are characterized as being of a certain number of words to the line. The two most widely used metres were the five-word and the seven-word, i.e. of lines containing respectively five or seven words. Virtually all Chinese poetry before the present century was rhymed; most common was the end-rhyming of even lines (i.e. lines 2, 4, 6, etc.). The *Songs*, although they do not show a constant length of line, have a predominantly four-word rhythm. Out of the *Songs* a completely regular four-word metre was developed during the Han, and this was fairly extensively employed up to the sixth century. Poets who used this regular four-word metre remained conscious of its origin and generally introduced many words and expressions, by then archaic, from the *Songs*. During the T'ang period (618–906) the five-word and the seven-word became the only normally used metres for *shih*-poetry, which they remained until the twentieth century. Both of these metres came into use for the first time during the Han, and here, once again, we meet with a problem for scholarly dispute in the matter of their origin. Once again the issue has been confused by the attribution of later work to earlier poets. *We plaited our hair* and *Resentful song* (pp. 5 and 6) are examples of such attribution. If such poems are excluded, rather thin material remains, but it does give a glimpse into the development of the new metres. A number of short popular songs or rhymed sayings, preserved in the *History of the Former Han dynasty*, provide evidence for their having had a popular origin. For example, there is the following popular song of the reign of the emperor Ch'êng (33–7 B.C.) in c. 27:

> Crooked paths spoil good fields,
> Slanderous mouths confound good men.
> The cassia tree's blossoms do not fruit;
> The yellow bird nests in its top.
> What formerly men envied,
> Now is what men pity.

(This owes its preservation to its having been thought to be a portent of the fall of the Former Han dynasty at the hand of Wang Mang.)

The rather stilted quality of poems in the five-word and seven-word metres by literary men of the first and early second centuries also seems to indicate uncertainty in the use of a new form. However by the later part of the second century the five-word, which until the T'ang period was generally more favoured than the seven-word, was being widely and fluently used.

In contrast to their unfavourable attitude towards the Han *fu*, modern Chinese critics have great praise for the Han songs,

known as *yüeh-fu*. This term *yüeh-fu* was originally the name of
the Bureau of Music, created during the reign of the Emperor
Wu in the second century B.C., with the task of collecting folk-
songs from various regions of the empire and of commissioning
new songs from well-known poets. It is known that the texts
of some hundreds of these folk-songs were collected in the Han
imperial library, but almost all have been lost. The great majority
of the Han popular *yüeh-fu* songs which have survived probably
come from the Later Han. While some number of the songs have
an irregular metrical pattern, which is preserved in later 'imita-
tions', many are in a regular five-word line. The exact signifi-
cance of this is not quite clear. It would seem that the growing
popularity of the five-word metre was influencing the *yüeh-fu* as
well as *shih*-poetry. Much stress has been laid upon the folk
character of the *yüeh-fu*. Yet there is no doubt that, whatever
their origin, these songs owe their preservation to the actions of
literary men, and in the process some slight measure of styliza-
tion may have occurred. In the latter part of the second century
there is often very little in form or content to distinguish *yüeh-fu*
from *shih*. By this time the *yüeh-fu* songs had made their par-
ticular contribution to the progress of poetry, a contribution
of simplicity and directness.

Being songs, the *yüeh-fu* tend to a certain generality in ex-
pression; the situations they treat, the emotions they portray,
are typical situations, common emotions. This of course does
not prevent their feelings from being sincere. The fine song *The
orphan* may serve as an illustration:

> An orphan to be born,
> An orphan to become,
> The fate is truly bitter.
>
> When my father and mother were alive,
> I rode a stout carriage,
> Drove four horses.

When my father and mother died,
My brother and my sister-in-law made me a trader.
South I went to Chiu-chiang,
East I went to Ch'i and Lu.
In the last month of the year I came home,
But dare not speak of my hardships.
My head was full of lice,
My face was covered with dust.
My elder brother told me to prepare a meal,
My sister-in-law told me to see to the horses.
Up I went to the high hall,
Then down again I ran to the hall below:
The orphan's tears fall like rain.

They sent me in the morning to draw water,
In the evening with the water I came home.
My hands were chapped,
I had no sandals on my feet.
Sadly I trod the frost,
With many thorns among it.
The thorns broke off in the flesh of my calves;
In my pain I wanted to weep.
My tears flowed continually,
Their clear drops unceasing.
In winter I had no padded coat,
In summer no unlined jacket.
Since alive, I was not happy,
It were better early to die
And go the Yellow Springs beneath the earth.

Spring air stirs,
Plants begin to sprout.
In the third month mulberry-leaves for silkworms,
In the sixth month harvesting the melons.
I took out the melon-cart
And started back home.
The melon-cart overturned.
Those who helped me were few,
Those who ate the melons were many.

'Please give me back the stalks.
My brother and sister-in-law are strict;
As soon as I get home,
They will make trouble.'

At home oh what an uproar!
I want to send a letter
To my father and mother beneath the earth:
'My brother and sister-in-law are hard to live with for long.'

The last forty years of the second century provided a great
stimulus to poetry. Politically they present an example of the
typical collapse of a great dynasty. The emperors were no longer
successfully fulfilling their theoretical role as the apex of the
bureaucratic organization. Real power was being disputed
among groups who had no standing in the theoretical constitu-
tion, e.g. the palace eunuchs, the families of imperial relatives by
marriage, and above all the 'great families', which, by building
up great wealth and lands, maintained a continuing political
power. Vast numbers of landless and distressed peasants swelled
the numbers of the adherents of the great landed families or the
ranks of banditry. Great peasant revolts occurred, and their sup-
pression brought into the power struggle successful military
commanders who could employ their armies to their own ends.
It was such a military leader Ts'ao Ts'ao who finally succeeded
Han in the possession of North China and whose son Ts'ao P'ei
formally established the dynasty of Wei. The literati of the
period also attempted to organize themselves, but theirs was the
most vulnerable group.

The shattering of the golden image of imperial grandeur, the
degeneration of Confucianism into a rather narrow scholasti-
cism and its apparent inability to offer new answers to the
political needs of the time, the continuous instability of social
life, all seem to have worked to turn the thinking individual in-
ward upon himself. The reaction to the collapse of the social

order was intensely pessimistic and escapist, but in so far as it promoted a consciousness of literature as a personal and individual expression of feeling, it was important. Poem fifteen of the famous anonymous series *Nineteen Old Poems*, which almost certainly date from this time, characterizes the prevailing attitude.

> Life's years do not fill a hundred,
> But always they embrace a thousand years' sorrows.
> Since day is short and bitter night long,
> Why not take a light and wander out?
> To be happy you must be abreast of the time,
> How can you wait for the years to come?
> The fool who grudges expense
> Is but later ages' laughter.
> With the immortal Wang-tzŭ Ch'iao
> It is hard to appoint a date.

In the *Nineteen Old Poems* it is possible to see the degree of perfection which the five-word *shih* had now achieved. As a literary form it was beginning to reach equality of standing with the *fu*.

With the turn of the second century China entered upon the long period of four centuries between the great dynasties of Han and T'ang, which has been called appropriately the Period of Disunity. The Han Empire broke up into the tripartite division of the Three Kingdoms, and, although a reunification took place in the latter part of the third century under the Western Chin, this ineffective dynasty was driven out of North China by the invading Huns in 316. Until the reconstitution of a unified empire by the Sui, who played a somewhat similar historical role towards the T'ang to that which Ch'in played in creating the institutional basis for Han, in 589, China remained divided between north and south. In the south the Chinese, confined to an area which was still largely a 'colonial' territory, lived under a series of weak dynasties of comparatively short duration, but all clinging to the legitimacy of their succession to the former

Chinese power; in the north barbarians of different stock set up states which for varying periods controlled parts or all of the Chinese homeland. Regarded from the standpoint of Chinese power and prestige, the Period of Disunity was not a happy age, but for our present topic it is very important. For in it so much of the essential character of Chinese poetry was fashioned. Literary criticism and literary classification made their appearance. In it the peculiar dangers in Chinese poetic treatment became apparent, the danger of too great a concentration on musical effect at the expense of content, the danger of the intellectual too heavily overbalancing the emotional, the danger of convention replacing observation. Poetry from this period onwards became closely associated not only with music but also with painting. This unity of the arts had its credit side. The simple and strong delineation of painting produced its counterpart in the strikingly economical, graphic description of landscape in verse. Yet it carried with it the danger that the poet looked with the painter's eye, and often did not bother to look at all, becoming content to substitute the pictorial representation for the actuality. In general, it may be fairly said that no poetry was to be so beset with the dangers of mannerisms as the Chinese. For it lived for so long, so greatly within its own traditions. The one major foreign cultural influence upon native tradition, Buddhism, began to have its greatest effect at the highest intellectual level within this Period of Disunity. From the fourth century on through most of the T'ang period it claimed the attention of many of the best minds. If we ask the difficult question of what the Buddhist infiltration added to Chinese mental attitudes, difficult because the early Chinese Buddhist converts themselves were able to discover analogies from Chinese tradition, we may find some answer in a heightened sense of spirituality and an increase in individualism. The political and social conditions of this period encouraged men's consciousness of themselves as individuals. The effect of Buddhism seems to have been to foster and promote this inherent tendency. Speaking more particularly, Buddhism can be said to have provided a spiritual basis for the art of landscape ('hills and streams') in painting and poetry. But here again it is hard to say that Buddhism provided the essential stimulus to the contemplation of landscape. The great difference in the physical conditions of the new Chinese environment in the south from the brown and dusty northern plains must itself have been of great influence.

In this period between Han and T'ang the conception of literature as an art to be pursued for its own sake without need of social or moral purpose was tacitly achieved, and the belief that a man might secure an enduring identity, a name as a writer, was entertained by individuals. Thus Liu Hsieh (465–522), the most famous of Chinese critics of any period, wrote in the preface to his *Wên-hsin tiao-lung* (*The Heart of Literature and the Carving of Dragons*): 'Years and months haste away, man's spirit does not endure, it is only by writing that a man may raise up his fame and give range to his deeds.' By this time the great poet (and in China, as elsewhere, the great poet is usually himself aware of his own greatness) could have an assurance of the survival of his name through his poetry. But, however great his fame as poet, his position in Chinese society, using the word in a broad not a narrow sense, depended on his achieving the rank of an official. In the Chinese system to gain literary reputation very usually brought some sort of official post in its train, if none had been earlier secured. For a writer of note never to have held a post, however humble, that might be attached to his name, nor at any rate to have the distinction of having declined a proffered appointment, is very rare in the history of Chinese literature. The great T'ang poet Li Po is the most famous exception. This social fact must partly explain the recurrent demand that literature should serve social ends. It is interesting to note that the times when literature is most clearly pursued for its own sake, when elaboration is at its height and the 'dragons' are most minutely carved, often correspond to periods of political decline. The Period of Disunity of the fourth to sixth centuries and the Late-T'ang and Five Dynasties period of the ninth and tenth centuries are excellent examples. Both are known as periods of excessive elaboration, and the periods which followed them are represented as ages not only of political but literary resurgence. Since the man of letters had so fortunate a position in the social hierarchy, he could hardly not contract some social obligations. It was the dual character of the literatus-politician which created for him this tension in his attitude to literature. It is therefore probably mistaken to think that poets or critics who enunciate the Confucian doctrine of the social role of poetry were merely uttering platitudes to which they gave no more than lip-service. This is to take too modern and too Western a viewpoint. So long as the traditional pattern of society persisted, this tension could never for long be unfelt, and it may well be that it acted as a very useful brake upon the very clever but very shallow aestheticism into which Chinese poetry could so easily run.

It may here be appropriate to notice one particular result of the place in society of Chinese poets. In almost any Chinese poet's collection one is immediately struck by the high proportion of poems addressed to friends and acquaintances. The 'address and answer' category of poem was well established in the Period of Disunity and is extensively represented in the sixth-century anthologies *Wên-hsüan* and *Yü-t'ai hsin-yung*. The Chinese poet as an official was a member of a club with exclusive but extensive membership. When we speak in English of 'the bond of poetry', we are, I suppose, thinking primarily in terms of a community of language. If a Chinese poet had used a similar phrase, he would probably have been thinking in terms of the fellowship of a particular group in society. This curious feeling of intimacy in poetry, which might extend not merely across generations but across centuries, is very striking. At its lowest level it might reduce poetry to a trivial pastime but at its highest it could raise it to an expression of great human affection. Here is a very obvious and direct example of the bond of sympathy across the centuries in *What a pity!* by Tu Fu (712–70) (*Tu Kung-pu shih*, c. 22, 8, Harvard-Yenching Concordance):

> The flowers fly—why so fast?
> As I grow old, I wish that spring would linger.
> What a pity that scenes of joy
> Came not all in my youth and prime!
> To set free the mind there must be wine,
> To send forth one's feelings nothing is better than poetry.
> This thought you, T'ao Ch'ien, would understand,
> But my life has come after your time.

Only slightly less direct is Lu Chao-lin (seventh century) as he too thinks of T'ao Yüan-ming (T'ao Ch'ien):

> In the southern gully the spring begins to flow clear;
> By the eastern hedge the chrysanthemums just now are fragrant,
> Turning my thoughts back to how, under the northern window,
> Serenely slept Hsi-huang.
>
> (*Yu-yu tzŭ chi*, SPTK, c. 3, 3a)

The transition from the chrysanthemums to the man is made because for every reader 'chrysanthemums by the eastern hedge' would immediately call to mind T'ao's famous fifth poem in his series *Drinking wine* (see p. 9).

'To send forth one's feelings nothing is better than poetry,' wrote Tu Fu. In the period between Han and T'ang the exchange of poems had become an established convention of literary-political society. Frequently the answering poem 'harmonized' with that received, that is the same rhyme-words were employed in it. This convention no doubt encouraged the use of the short *shih*-poem in the expression of feelings that were immediate and personal. For taking leave of a friend, for the impromptu verse of the social meeting, long and sustained forms were clearly not appropriate. It seems then fairly obvious that the social character of so much verse composition forwarded the tendency towards the short poem which is immediately re-marked as a general characteristic of Chinese verse. It follows too that such short poems did not set forth grand themes, though the enduring problems of man's life might be suggestively glanced at in the treatment of a particular situation. The very nature of the classical language with its lack of inflexion tended always to give a generality of expression. Though at no period was all poetic writing made up of such social verse, it formed so great a part as to exercise a decisive influence over the whole. The similarity of education and traditions which most poets shared, added to the strong impulse towards short poems, pro-duced the almost inevitable result of allusiveness, suggestion, and other devices to secure the maximum expression within the poem's small compass. All these features make a great amount of later Chinese poetry difficult to appreciate fully from the outside, and the translator for the general Western reader, particularly if he is selecting a few poems only from a large number of poets, is constrained to choose examples with an apparently universal sound or to gloss over and dissolve allusions. In fact more detailed study often shows the apparently straightforward to possess its subtleties. Thus there must arise some conflict be-tween the historical study of Chinese poetry and the desire to give the Western reader renderings of Chinese poems.

Throughout the fourth, fifth, and sixth centuries the *shih*-poem came, at first to challenge, and gradually to usurp the position of the *fu* as the main vehicle of literary poetry. Also extensively used was the *yüeh-fu* song. Many of these songs bear the same titles as, or are specifically declared to be in imitation of, old Han songs; others were written to current tunes. But as a general rule they are written in regular five or seven-word metres, though their prototypes may be of an irregular line. Thus formally the *yüeh-fu* of this period seldom appear very different from *shih*; it is in their content that some distinction can be made. The *yüeh-fu* was commonly used by poets for the more general theme, the standard themes on which every poet must express himself. Here is Pao Chao (*c.* 420–66) writing on the perennial subject of man's decline to the tune *From youth to declining age*:

> I recall how before, in the time of my youth,
> I galloped off, delighting in the bright dawn.
> I formed friendships with many noble families,
> Went in and out among wealthy neighbours.
> Thin silks' seductive, gay show,
> Carriages and horses raising a dust,
> Girls of Ch'ing and Ch'i singing,
> Men of Yen and Chao plucking the lute,
> Excellent wine full of fragrant flavours,
> The taste of delicacies spoiling foods in season,
> Nowadays whenever I think of them,
> These things are remote and of no consequence.
> I say to you who come after,
> To make merry you must catch the spring.

(On p. 20 Po Chü-i may be seen using 'Grand ode' for somewhat similar sentiments.)

Pao Chao is a poet who receives honourable mention in current Chinese works, because it is possible to find, in his poetry, lines which show sympathy with the lot of the common people, and it is claimed that he was influenced by folk-song. A more dispassionate examination of the language of his poetry reveals him as no less literary than other poets of the period. He was one of the first to be attracted by the personality of T'ao Yüan-ming and to express his sense of affinity by conscious echoes and imitations. If some of the songs which Pao 'imitated' were current folk songs, it is not very easy to measure the extent of their influence. For there are no originals to set against his work, and even if we had originals transmitted through literary sources, whether they retained their true popular character would remain doubtful. So much of what is claimed to be of popular origin in early Chinese literature seems to show the imprint of sophistication. This is perhaps partly true of the *Wu Songs*, which are acclaimed as very beautiful popular songs of this period and which the great T'ang poet Li Po used as a song form to which to set new words. It is clear from the number preserved that these simple, often playful love-songs had a great vogue at this time. To give one example:

> The ice in the pool is three feet thick,
> White snow covers a thousand *li*.
> My heart is like the pine and cypress,[1]
> But what is your heart like?

One may see in such examples (the *Wu Songs* are all quatrains) a foreshadowing of the four-line *chüeh-chü* or 'cut-short' poem which reached perfection under the T'ang.

The *chüeh-chü* was a particular form of the 'regulated' poem (*lü-shih*), also called the 'new-style' poem to distinguish it from the unregulated or 'old' form. The final perfecting of the 'regulated' forms was done in the early part of the T'ang period, but the ground-work was laid in the last hundred or so years of the southern dynasties.[2] While reacting against the alleged floridness and lack of content of 'Ch'i-Liang' (the southern dynasties which ruled 479–556), T'ang poets did not reject the achievements of this period in the matter of form. The features of the regulated poem were a precisely balanced parallelism of phrasing between the lines of the poem and a selection of words to produce an ordered pattern of tonal sound. Parallelism is a feature which may be regarded as endemic in the nature of the classical Chinese language, but the conscious approach to

1. Symbol of constancy.
2. Though I have referred mainly to the south during the Period of Disunity, the same general tendencies were followed by Chinese or by sinified foreign poets in the north.

literature of this period developed parallelism in both prose and verse as a deliberate effect. The translation of Buddhist sutras into Chinese and the recitation of these sutras seem to have made the Chinese more conscious of the tonal qualities of their language. The period between Han and T'ang saw the appearance of a number of studies upon the subject. The formulation of tonal theory in poetry is especially ascribed to Shên Yüeh (441–513), who is said to have pointed out eight faults or undesirable tonal combinations. If Shên Yüeh can be regarded as the prime mover, the progress to the *lü-shih* patterns, which became standard from the T'ang period onwards, was gradual, extending over about two centuries. The perfected *lü-shih* patterns are a careful balancing of contrasted level (where the voice remains at the same pitch), and oblique (where the voice either rises or falls) tones. The normal *lü-shih* in either the five or seven-word metre was of eight lines; the 'cut-short' (*chüeh-chü*) form was of but four. The reader will find a good many examples of this neat vehicle for virtuosity in the pages of this anthology. The Chinese never wearied of the attempt to trap the moment's vision in the net of four lines and many of their best-loved poems are to be found among the millions of *chüeh-chü* which have been written since the seventh century.

So we come from the period of preparation for T'ang to the 'golden age' itself. The question above all to be asked is the question: why? For it is surely no mere accident of time that Li Po, Tu Fu, and Po Chü-i, whom any Chinese would include in the first eight greatest Chinese poets, were all born in the eighth century. These three great names are supported by a host of minor ones. In the preceding pages I have tried to show that the centuries before had developed the means and conditions for the poetic greatness of T'ang, and, although T'ang poets were given to regarding their immediate predecessors as decadents who had lost the Way of poetry, their actual debt to them is patent. We find among poets the same call for a return to anti-

quity as that which in prose-writing produced the so-called
ku-wên ('old-style') movement. The situation of prose and
poetry, however, was not the same. Han Yü, the great *ku-wên*
advocate, might urge the return to the prose models of Chou and
Han, but poetry obviously could not return to the *Book of Songs*
for its model. Poets could only repeat the principles which the
early Confucians had established out of the *Book of Songs*: that
poetry ought to have a political and moral purpose. Some poets
did try to put these principles into deliberate practice, but on the
whole they perhaps remained no more than a psychological
nagging of which the effect is hard to estimate. Confucianism
did not indeed recover its dominant position in the intellectual
centre of society during T'ang, when both Buddhism and
Taoism show a pervasive vitality. The great Confucian revival
was still to come in the eleventh and twelfth centuries under the
Sung dynasty. Nevertheless, in the sphere of political organiza-
tion, Confucian ideas did have important effect with the restora-
tion of the examination system as a means of entry into the
bureaucracy. The T'ang examinations, which set the general
form which was to persist up to the end of the Manchu period,
were based upon knowledge of the Confucian canonical books,
but included the composition of a *shih*-poem. Hence arose the
neat saying that 'T'ang obtained officials (*shih*) by poems (*shih*)'
and the belief that the great age of T'ang poetry was due to the
examination system. While it is easy to dismiss such an idea on
the ground that examination poems were usually not very good
poems, this is to ignore the more general effect of the examina-
tions. They did of course encourage learning, even if of a narrow
and specialized kind, but more importantly they fostered a great
sense among the examination candidates of comradeship and also
of being an élite. Politically, those who gained office through the
examination entry were, as a group weak when compared with
those other groups which in T'ang, as at other periods, dis-
rupted the ideal constitution, great families, eunuchs, military

leaders, and so on, but the prestige attached to becoming a *chin-shih*, a successful candidate in the metropolitan literary examination, was maintained. The examinations did therefore attract and bring together men of literary talents. On the one hand this promoted the social tendency of Chinese verse which has already been noted, on the other it did perhaps bring greater numbers of poets and writers into contact with one another. In general one may probably say that for the T'ang poet the world seemed wider than for the poets of the preceding period, society was more open. Poetry was greatly honoured, and it was always reaching a wider audience. Finally, poetry was written with ease and assurance, and by the great with greatness, because poets were not in doubt over the fitness of their work for the time.

It is customary to divide T'ang poetry into four periods, the early period of the seventh century, the high period of the first part of the eighth century to which Li Po and Tu Fu belong, the mid-T'ang period of the later eighth and the beginning of the ninth century to which Po Chü-i belongs, and the Late-T'ang period to the end of the dynasty in 907. As has been already said, Late-T'ang parallels the last century of the Period of Disunity in becoming over-interested in the verbal effects of poetry at the expense of content: it has, as Chinese critics express it, 'sounds but no bone'. With this similarity of tendency, it also developed a new poetical form rather in the way that Ch'i and Liang developed the *lü-shih*. This new form, which was a song lyric, is most commonly known by the name *tz'ǔ* ('words'), but also by the old name *yüeh-fu*, *ch'ang-tuan chü* ('long and short lines', i.e. irregular verse), or *shih-yü*, which means 'the last development of the *shih*'. Much has been written upon the origin of this irregular verse form. The problem has been slightly complicated by the desire to have too tidy a beginning for this new form. This desire may be said to have earlier and more recent manifestations. The earlier manifestation was in the attempt to find an appropriate founder for the form in the poet Li Po. Li Po used the old *yüeh-fu* forms extensively and perhaps thus seemed a suitable poet to have created a new song form. Whereas the *yüeh-fu* had long become a matter of adapting or writing new words for existing song-libretti, the appearance of the *tz'ŭ* essentially marks a new attempt to write song words more directly to particular tunes. The *tz'ŭ*, like the older *yüeh-fu*, had often no other title than the name of the tune to which they were written. The practice of entitling *tz'ŭ* by tune-names continued (and is continued by those who compose *tz'ŭ* today) after the *tz'ŭ*-patterns had in their turn become standardized and might be looked up in a reference book. (The *tz'ŭ* have tonal patterns like those of the *lü-shih*.) In many *tz'ŭ*-anthologies there are ascribed to Li Po poems entitled by tunes which do not appear to have become current until some considerable time after his death. Thus it looks as if Li Po's founding of the art of *tz'ŭ*-writing has been doubtfully advocated. In a different manner some modern writers seem to try to pinpoint too exactly the time in which the *tz'ŭ* begins. Since there are cases where either the old classification *yüeh-fu* or the new classification *tz'ŭ* can be applied, it is perhaps reasonable to see a gradual transition from the one to the other, as poets became interested in writing for a variety of new tunes, many of which are said to have come into the T'ang repertoire from Central Asia. By Late-T'ang, the *tz'ŭ* form was recognizably distinct and had found its first great master in Wên T'ing-yün.

The chief aims of the early *tz'ŭ* are sound and colour. The graphic effect is produced by a series of rapid and broken strokes: there is an almost entire absence of grammatical construction, no attempt to link the changes of focus. A very literal translation of one of Wên T'ing-yün's *tz'ŭ* may give some impression of the original technique. This is to the tune *The waterclock*:

> Jade incense-burner's fragrance,
> Red candle's tears,
> Unevenly light the decorated chamber's sadness.

Eyebrows' black thin,
Tresses' clouds fallen:
Night long, coverlet and pillow cold.

Wu-t'ung trees,
Third watch rain,
Care not for separation's sorrow's utter bitterness.
Single leaf by leaf,
Single sound by sound,
On the empty steps dripping until dawn.

(*Hua-chien chi*, SPPY, C. I, 4b)

There are many such lonely women waiting for lovers who do
not come among the early *tz'ŭ*: the red candles continually
gutter. Poets' association with singing-girls had some part in the
tz'ŭ's ancestry. The *tz'ŭ* comes closest to 'pure poetry' in the
current use of the word 'pure'. It made little use of literary
allusions and admitted the colloquial idiom of the day. The
translator is, with the *tz'ŭ*, less liable to be thwarted by the poet's
erudition, but he has to counter the difficulty presented by the
technique of expression. The present anthology gives a wide
representation of this form.

The analogy between the *tz'ŭ* and the *lü-shih* is well sustained
by the subsequent history. While Sung condemned the deca-
dence of Late-T'ang, just as T'ang had previously condemned
Ch'i and Liang, it retained and brought into wider use the *tz'ŭ*
form which was so obviously the result of the aestheticism of
Late-T'ang. The Sung indeed became the great age of *tz'ŭ*, and
modern Chinese historians may give all the space which they
devote to Sung poetry to this one form. Historically this must
seem unsound, since hardly any of the major Sung poets ex-
pressed themselves mainly through this form. To confine one-
self to the *tz'ŭ* of Su Shih, who showed greatness in whatever
form he handled, is like reading only the sonnets of Words-
worth and ignoring all his other poetry. For the *tz'ŭ* in the Sung
period, though then reaching its peak of development, had for

this very reason become but one of the forms the poet had to hand. The emphasis of the modern Chinese historian is stimulated by the slightly more popular character of the *tz'ŭ*, which popular character is enhanced by the reflection of the Chinese opera which was also beginning to take shape in the Sung period. The *tz'ŭ* provided the form for the arias of opera, which were, for the author, the part of importance; little concern was felt for the action and the story, and so for the prose sections which might be necessary to carry the story along. Of all the literature from the thirteenth century onwards, little but the opera and the novel occupy the modern Chinese literary historian. In the more extreme cases one feels the feeblest opera may receive more attention than the best poetry in the literary language. There is certainly much good poetry to be found in operatic arias, but to translate single arias is after all to prise out gems from their setting, loosely cemented though they may be, for the construction of the Chinese opera is notably loose by our dramatic standards. The translation of a whole opera inevitably loses all the colour and sound of actual performance: one guesses that Chinese seldom read operas. Our present translators have in this later period made their selection only from poetry in the *shih* and *tz'ŭ* forms and have shown that there is no diminution of quality. It is very hard for us to conceive of a period of 700 years of poetic activity without the creation of new forms, a period not only without the influence of any considerable external stimuli but also with an ever-present consciousness of the great models of its own past. The wonder is that any poet could escape from the most sterile imitation in the close confines of the Chinese manner which generally found little place for unusual diction. Yet there is perhaps little evidence that the Chinese were oppressed by the weight of their traditions before the period of intensive contact with the West over the last eighty years.

The twentieth century has drawn a heavy line across the time-chart of Chinese culture. Revolution has come in poetry as elsewhere. There are many Chinese who publicly or privately dismiss the new poetry as so much tuneless rubbish, and some, including Chairman Mao, have continued to write pleasantly in the traditional metres and with more or less of the traditional manner. To such persons the T'ang dynasty still does not seem very far off, but the gap cannot be prevented from growing. After the Literary Revolution the writing of new poetry began in an atmosphere of great uncertainty (Hu Shih called his attempts appropriately enough *Experiments*) but of some excitement. In the nineteen-twenties every Western metre was tried as well as sundry modifications of native forms. Rhymeless verse, unknown to the Chinese ear, appeared, and poems sometimes sported foreign words in the middle of their characters to match Ezra Pound's efforts in the reverse direction. One noticeable break with tradition was a tendency towards longer poems. This period is of great interest and awaits study by a sinologist with a wide knowledge and appreciation of contemporary Western writing and art. Such a person will be hard to find. The task is a very difficult one. For it is actually more difficult to achieve an appreciation of Chinese which sounds like English than of Chinese which does not. Over the past twenty-five years poetry, like other literary forms in China, has been firmly harnessed to the propaganda machine through the war with Japan, the civil war, the cold war, the numerous campaigns and plans of the last decade. It is idle to pretend that there is not much here which must seem either hostile or ludicrous to most Western readers. The important test of sincerity is hard to apply. It can only be said that in the brief period of the Hundred Flowers (1957) it was declared that literature was being destroyed by stereotypes. Though such criticisms were soon silenced, there is some comfort in their not all having been made by the very old.

University of Sydney   A. R. DAVIS

CHRONOLOGICAL TABLE OF
CHINESE HISTORICAL PERIODS

Legendary period
The Five Emperors   3rd millennium B.C.
Hsia dynasty   *c.* 21st–16th century B.C.

Shang dynasty   *c.* 16th–11th century B.C.

Chou dynasty   11th century–221 B.C.
Spring and Autumn period 722–481 B.C.
Warring States period   5th–3rd centuries B.C.

Ch'in dynasty   221–06 B.C.

Han dynasty   206 B.C.–A.D. 220
Former Han   206 B.C.–A.D. 9
Usurpation of Wang Mang A.D. 9–24
Later Han   A.D. 25–220

The Three Kingdoms   220–80

Western Chin dynasty   265–316

Period of division between north
 and south   317–589

Sui dynasty   581–617

T'ang dynasty   618–907

The Five Dynasties   907–59

Sung dynasty   960–1279
Northern Sung   960–1126
Southern Sung   1127–1279

Yüan (Mongol) dynasty   1280–1367

Ming dynasty   1368–1644

Ch'ing (Manchu) dynasty   1644–1911

Republic of China   1912–
People's Republic of China 1949–

This rude door

By this rude door
I can abide in peace;
By this running stream
I can gladly endure hunger.

Why for a meal of fish
Must I have River bream?
Why for a wife to wed
Must I have a beauty of Ch'i?

Why for a meal of fish
Must I have River carp?
Why for a wife to wed
Must I have a beauty of Sung?

The rain is not controlled

Vast and mighty Heaven,
Why withhold thy goodness,
Sending down death and famine,
Ravaging the four quarters of the land?
Great[1] Heaven, in thy majesty,
Why no concern, why no plan?
Regarding not the guilty
Who have suffered for their crimes,
Why are the guiltless
Swallowed up in wide calamities?

Why, mighty Heaven,
Does the king not hearken to righteous words,
Like one wandering afar
Unknowing of his goal?
Let all those in authority
Attend to their proper conduct.
If they fear not other men
Have they no fear for Heaven?

What plant is not yellow?

WHAT plant is not yellow?
What day is without a march?
What man is not on the move
Serving in the four quarters?

What plant is not black?
What man is not wifeless?
Heigho, for us soldiers!
We alone are not treated as men.

Not rhinoceroses, not tigers,
Yet we are loosed in this mighty waste.
Heigho, for us soldiers!
Day and night we never rest.

The fox with his broad brush
Lurks among the gloomy grass;
But our wagon with its bamboo body,
Rumbles along the road of Chou.

CH'IN CHIA

To my wife

1

MAN's life is like the morning dew:
In this world he has misfortune in plenty.
Griefs and hardships oft come early;
Glad unions oft come bitterly late.
Mindful that I had soon to leave on service,
Farther and farther away from you every day,
I sent a carriage to bring you back;
But it went empty, and empty it returned.
I read your letter with feelings of distress;
At meals I cannot eat;
And I sit alone in this desolate chamber.
Who is there to solace and encourage me?
Through the long nights I cannot sleep,
And solitary I lie prostrate on my pillow, tossing and
    turning.
Sorrow comes as in a circle
And cannot be rolled up like a mat.

2

EAGER, eager the charioteers prepare to journey;
Clang, clang, resound the bells.
At dawn they will lead me afar;
I fastened on my girdle to await cockcrow.
I peered into the empty room,
And my mind seemed to see your face and form.
One separation breeds ten thousand regrets;
Rising and sitting I am unquiet.
How am I to express my heart?
It is by these gifts as sincere tokens.

The precious hairpin is fit to add lustre to your hair;
The bright mirror will reflect your face;
The perfumes will help to cleanse;
And the plain lute holds clear notes.

The man in the *Song*,[1] grateful for the present of the
 quince,
Longed to send back a precious gem.
Abashed by your bounteous gifts,
I blush to let these trifles go forth.
But, though I know that they are but a poor return,
They have their value in showing my feelings.

HSÜ SHU[2]

To my husband

HAPLESS am I! •
In sickness I came here.
I am lingering within these doors,
For, though time passes, I remain uncured.
I neglect attention to you;
I break the laws of love and duty.
Now you, sir, to obey orders,
Have gone to the far-off Capital.
Long, long will be our separation,
And there is no way to tell you my thoughts.
Expecting your return I am all eagerness
And waiting for you, I stand about aimlessly.
My thoughts of you are knotted in my heart;
In sleep I think of your radiant countenance.
You have gone far away;
Your separation from me is daily lengthening.

4

Would that I had wings,
That I might fly after you.
Oft do I moan, and deep do I sigh,
And tears wet my coat.

From THE NINETEEN OLD POEMS

Green, green the river-side grass

GREEN, green the river-side grass,
Dense, dense the garden willows,
Fair, fair the girl upstairs,
Bright, bright she faces the casement,
Gay, gay her red-powdered face,
Slender, slender the white hand she extends.

Sometime a singing-girl,
Now she is a traveller's wife;
The traveller has departed and returns not,
And a mateless bed is hard to keep alone.

? SU WU

We plaited our hair

WE plaited our hair and became man and wife;
The love of us two was never in doubt.
Let us enjoy the bliss of tonight,
Making merry while the good time lasts.
But the far traveller must bethink him of the long road.
I rise to look what of the night:
Orion has already set.
Away, away! It is time for farewell.
I must take my place at the battlefront,

And for our next meeting there is no date.
A hand-clasp, a deep sigh,
And copious tears for a living separation.
Strive to enjoy Spring's flowers,
But forget not the time of our happiness.
Living, I will be sure to return;
Dead, I will be sure to think for ever of you.

? PAN CHIEH-YÜ

Resentful song

WHITE silk of *Ch'i*, newly torn out,
Spotlessly pure as the frozen snow,
Cut to make a fan of conjoined happiness,
Round as the moon at its brightest.
It is ever in and out my master's sleeve,
And its movement makes a gentle breeze.
But oft I fear with the Autumn's coming
When cold blasts drive away the torrid heat,
It will be cast aside into a chest,
And love in mid-course will end.

TS'AO TS'AO

« *Bitter cold* »

ON the North we ascend the T'ai-hang mountain,[1]
Dangerous and so high!
The Yang-ch'ang[2] slope is so rough and crooked
That it breaks the cart wheels.
How bare and desolate are the trees!
The north wind soughs mournful!

The bears crouch before us;
Tigers and leopards flank our path with their roaring;
The mounting passes have but few dwellers.
How fast the snow falls!
I stretch my neck with a deep sigh;
Marching afar, memories are many.
How sad and disconsolate is my heart!
I long to take one journey back eastward,
But the waters are deep and the bridges broken.
In the way I wander irresolute,
And in my bewilderment I have lost my old track.
Night falls and there is nowhere to lodge.
Marching, marching, more distant every day,
Men and horses alike are famished.
Men shoulder sacks to gather firewood,
And axe-hewn ice is for our gruel.
Sad is that song of the Eastern Mountains,[1]
For ever causing me sorrow.

HSÜ KAN

A wife's thoughts, III[2]

FLOATING clouds, how vast, how vast!
Would that through them I could send my tidings.
They drift and drift, and none can be sent,
And it is vain to linger here and pine.
Others part but reunite;
Only for you is there no date of return.
Since you, sir, went away,
My bright mirror is dim and untended.
My thoughts of you are like flowing water;
Will they ever have an end?

CHANG HUA

Yearnings, V

My eyes stray beyond the four corners of the wilderness;
At ease I tarry alone.
The orchids fringe a clear stream;
A wealth of flowers covers the green islets.
My fair one is not here –
If I plucked them to whom can I give them?
Birds in their nests know the wind's chill;
Beasts in their caves feel the sunless rain.
But if you have never endured far separation,
How can you know the yearning for an absent friend?

T'AO YÜAN-MING

(T'AO CH'IEN)

Returning to live in the country, I

In my youth I was out of tune with the common folk:
My nature is to love hills and mountains.
In my folly I fell into the net of the world's dust,
And so went on for thirty years.
The caged bird longs for its old woodland;
The pond-reared fish yearns for its native stream.
I have opened up a waste plot of the south moor,
And keeping my simplicity returned to garden and field.
A homestead of some ten acres,
A thatched cottage with eight or nine rooms;
Elms and willows shading the hinder eaves;
Peach and plum trees ranking before the hall.

8

Dim, dim is the distant hamlet;
Lagging, lagging hangs the smoke of the market-town;
A dog barks in the deep lane;
A cock crows on the top of the mulberry tree.
My door and courtyard have no dust and turmoil;
In the bare rooms there is leisure and to spare.
Too long a captive in a cage,
I have now come back to Nature.

Drinking wine, V

I BUILT my hut amid the throng of men,
But there is no din of carriages or horses.
You ask me how this can be.
When the heart is remote, earth stands aloof.
Culling chrysanthemums by the eastern hedge,
I see afar the southern hills;
The air of the hills at sunset is good;
The flying birds in company come back to their nests.
In this is the real savour,
But, probing, I can find no words.

LU K'AI

To Fan Yeh[1]

I HAVE plucked this plum-branch as I met a courier,
And send it to one at Lung-t'ou
South of the River I possess nothing;
My only gift is this single twig of Spring.

WANG JUNG

In imitation of Hsü Kan

Since you, sir, went away,
My golden burner has had no incense,
For thinking of you I am like the bright candle,
At midnight vainly burning itself away.

FAN YÜN

In imitation of 'Since you, sir, went away'[1]

Since you, sir, went away,
My gauze curtains sigh in the autumn's wind.
My thoughts of you are like the creeping grass
That grows and spreads without end.

T'AO HUNG-CHING

In reply to the Emperor's[2] *inquiry:*
'among the hills what have you?'

'Among the hills, what have I?'
On the ridges there are many white clouds;
But these are only for my own enjoyment –
They cannot be caught and sent on to your Majesty.

EMPEROR YANG OF SUI
(YANG KUANG)

Late spring

HERE in Loyang Spring tarries:
In all quarters there is Spring's radiance in plenty.
The willow-leaves are beginning to fade;
The peach-blossoms are falling but not yet scarce;
Spying under the eaves the swallows quarrel for entry;
Deep in the woods the birds fly in disorder.
But for those on duty at the frontier passes,
The steaming dew even now soaks their garments.

THE LADY HOU

Adornment ended

MY adornment is ended, but this only adds to my
    misery;
To dream of happiness is in itself a grief.
I have not even the choice of the willow-blossom
That can fly hither and thither when Spring comes.

YÜ SHIH-NAN

The cicada

IT lowers its head to drink the pure dew,
And its sound flows through the sparse T'ung trees;
For perched on high its voice, unaided, spreads afar,
And needs no help from the Autumn Wind.

11

WANG CHI

Passing the wine-seller's, II

In these days I am ever befuddled with wine,
But it is not for nourishing my nature and soul.
When I see that all men are drunk,
How can I bear to be the only one sober?

SUNG CHIH-WÊN

Crossing the Han river

Beyond the mountain there came no tidings and
    letters;
Winter passed, and then went Spring.
As I near my village my heart grows more afraid,
And I dare not inquire of those that come to meet me.

SU T'ING

*Inscribed on the wall of my small garden
as I was about to go to I-chou[1]*

The year is ended, and it only adds to my age;
Spring has come, but I must take leave of my home.
Alas, that the trees in this eastern garden,
Without me, will still bear flowers.

CHANG CHIU-LING

Since you, sir, went away[1]

SINCE you, sir, went away,
I have not returned to tend my fading loom,
For thinking of you I am like the moon at the full,
    That nightly wanes and loses its bright splendour.

WANG WEI

Mêng-ch'êng hollow[2]

MY new home is at the entrance to Mêng-ch'êng;
Of the old trees there remain only some fading willows.
After me who will be here?
It is vain to grieve that others had it before me.

LI PO

To Wang Lun

I HAD gone aboard and was minded to depart,
When suddenly I heard from the shore your song with
    tap of foot.
The Peach-blossom Pool[3] is a thousand feet deep,
But not so deep as the love in your farewell to me.

Question and answer among the mountains

You ask me why I dwell in the green mountain;
I smile and make no reply for my heart is free of care.
As the peach-blossom flows down stream and is gone
    into the unknown,
I have a world apart that is not among men.

Drinking with a recluse among the mountains

The two of us drink face to face where the mountain
    blossoms open;
Another cup, another cup, again another cup.
I am bemused and long to drowse; depart my friend;
Tomorrow at morn, if you are so minded, clasp your
    lute and come.

« Pure peace music »

The mist is deep, the waters are broad;
Tidings and letters have no way to reach him.
Only in the azure sky there is the moon beyond the
    clouds,
Minded to shine on the love-lorn pair so far apart.
All day things remind me and wound my heart;
My sad eyebrows are like a lock that's hard to open.
Night after night I ever keep for him the half of my
    quilt
In expectation of his spirit coming back to me in a
    dream.

TU FU

A moonlit night[1]

THIS night at Fu-chou in moonlight,
In her chamber she alone looks out;
Afar I pity my little children
That they know not yet to think of Ch'ang-an.
In the sweet mist her cloud-like tresses are damp;
In the clear moonlight her jade-like arms are cold.
When shall we two nestle against those unfilled curtains,
With the moon displaying the dried tear-stains of us both?

A visitor has come[2]

(Rejoicing that Magistrate Ts'ui has come to see me)

SOUTH of the house, north of the house, everywhere the
    water of Spring;
I can see only the flocks of gulls that arrive day after
    day.
The flowery path has not yet been swept for a guest,
The wicker-gate is only today opened for you.
For supper I am too far from market to add a dish;
For the bottle in a poor house there is only stale wine.
If you are willing to drink with an old neighbour of mine,
I will call over the hedge to finish off the wine with him.

.

To General Hua[1]

In the City of Brocade the lutes and the pipes all day
    make riot;
Half of the music is lost in the river breezes, and half in
    the clouds.
But this song should only belong to heaven;
Among mortals how seldom can it be heard!

TS'ÊN SHÊN

*Seeing the Wei river while travelling west through
Wei-chou and thinking of Ch'in-ch'uan*

The water of the Wei River flows away eastward –
When will it reach Yungchow?
I use it to add a double stream of tears,
And send them flowing down to my old home.

A spring dream

In the depth of my chamber last night the breeze of
    Spring arose;
My old friend and I are still parted by the waters of the
    Hsiang River.
On my pillow, in a flash of time, came Spring's dream,
Wherein I covered all the thousand miles of Chiang-nan.

SSŬ-K'UNG SHU

At the riverside village

MY fishing done, I have returned, but do not moor my boat;
At the riverside village the moon will set just as I go to
sleep.
Even if during the night the wind wafts me away,
I shall only reach the shallows where the rushes bloom.

WEI YING-WU

Night

THE light, where does it go?
The darkness, whence does it come?
Only do I know that of my ageing year by year
One half herein is sped.

MÊNG CHIAO

« *Wanderer's song* »

THE thread from a fond mother's hand
Is now in the jacket of her absent son.
As his departure came near, closer and closer was the
stitching.
Her mind fearing that his return would be delayed and
delayed.
Who says that the heart of an inch-long plant
Can requite the radiance of full Spring?

HAN YÜ

Snow in Spring

THE new year has yet no fragrant blossoms,
But the second moon suddenly sees the grass sprouting;
The white snow, vexed by the late coming of Spring's
  colours,
Of set purpose darts among the courtyard's trees to
  fashion flying petals.

CHANG CHI

« Song of a chaste wife », to the Ssŭ-k'ung Li Shih-tao[1]

You knew sir, that I had a husband,
When you sent me this pair of shining pearls.
Grateful for your skein-soft thoughts,
I wore them over my red gauze bodice.
But my home is a tall house built beside the Imperial
  grounds,
And my good man bears arms in the Palace of Radiance.
I know, sir, that your heart is pure as the sun and the
  moon.
But in serving my husband I have vowed to be with
  him in life and death;
So I now return your two shining pearls with a tear on
  each,
Regretting that we did not meet while I was still unwed.

Autumn thoughts

HERE in Loyang City as I felt the Autumn wind,
I longed to write home, but my thoughts were
    countless.
I feared that in my haste I had not said all,
And, as the messenger made to go, I broke the seal again.

YANG CHÜ-YÜAN

East of the city in early spring

FOR the poet the purest aspect is at new Spring,
When the willow's yellow has not yet equalled its green.
If I wait till the flowers of Shanglin Park[1] are like
    brocade,
All men would go out of doors to see the flowers.

PO CHÜ-I

Idly gazing from the southern pavilion
while on sick leave

LEANING on my pillow, away from my office,
With doors closed for two days,
At last I understand that in the service of the State,
It is only in sickness that a man has leisure.
Leisurely thoughts depend not on space,
For this small summer-house is but ten feet square.
Yet above the western eaves and the bamboo tips,
Without rising I can see the T'ai-po[2] mountains.
I blush afar that the clouds on the hill-tops
Should look down on this face with its dust of toil.

« Grand ode »

THE heavens are lasting and the earth endures without
    an end:
Yesternight, this morning, and again tomorrow.
My hair is grey and my teeth gape asunder.
Unknowing I have come to my forty-seventh year;
Going on to fifty – how many years remain?
I hold up my mirror, and seeing my face I am troubled.
Since I have no long rope to tie up the white sun,
And since I have no potent drug to keep my rosy
    cheeks,
Those rosy cheeks day by day suffer a slow change.
Where are the glories of the Green History?[1]
We wish to keep our youth and wait for wealth and
    honour,
But wealth and honour come not, and youth departs –
Departs and again departs like the Long River
Flowing eastward to the sea with no returning waves.
Good and bad, noble and base, all come to the same end:
On Pei-mang[2] the graves rise on high.
From the beginning all has been thus, and I am not
    alone in this;
Until death comes there is wine, so I raise my voice in
    song.
Yen Hui's[3] life was short; Po I[4] went hungry;
What I have attained already is much.
For glory, riches and honour we must abide our Fate;
If Fate comes not, how can we do aught to help?

« Secret parting »

THERE can be no tears
For a secret farewell;
There can be no converse
For a hidden love.
Besides our two hearts no man can know it;
Locked deep in its cage by night the lonely bird rests.
The keen sword in Spring sunders the twining branches;
The water of the river, though muddy, may yet become clear;
The head of the crow, though black, may yet become
    white.
But for a secret farewell and for a hidden love,
The two must be content to hope for naught to come.

Leaving my thatched cottage, III

THREE thatched cottages open on the hill;
One strip of mountain stream girds my home.
Colours of Mountain, Sounds of Stream, show no distress!
When my three years of public office are over I shall
    return to you.

Sighing for myself

FEASTING and travel, sleep and food, in time lose their
    savour;
Wine-cups and flutes and fiddles but entangle the body.
My guests are happy, my servants are well-fed;
At last I know that official rank profits only others.

YÜAN CHÊN

Expression of my grief
(Three poems)

1

HER father loved best his youngest daughter;
After she married me in poverty she had a hundred
    devices.
When I lacked clothes, she sought in her wicker-box;
When I wanted to buy wine, I coaxed her to pull out
    her golden hairpin.
Wild plants were our food, and long beans tasted sweet;
Fallen leaves from an old locust-tree added to our fuel.
Today my official pay is more than a hundred thousand,
But for you I can only make pious offering.

2

IN the past we jested of widowhood;
Today it has come before my eyes.
Your clothes have nearly all been given away;
But the needlework still remains that I cannot bear to
    uncover.
I yet remember the old affection, and am kind to maids
    and men,
And for that dream I have given away money.
I know that this sorrow is the lot of all,
But when man and wife have shared poverty a hundred
    things bring grief.

3

IDLY I sit in grief for myself and in grief for you,
How much time is a hundred years?[1]
Têng Yu,[2] childless, understood his fate;

P'an Yüeh,[1] mourning for his wife, still wrote poems to
    her.
To share a grave's darkness where is my hope?
In another life to meet again is yet harder to expect.
Only for the whole night my eyes are ever open
To requite you for a lifetime of knitted brows.

CHIA TAO

Knight-errant

For ten years this sword has been whetted,
But its frost-white blade has not yet been tried.
Today I grasp it to show it to you –
Who has any wrongs to requite?

P'EI I-CHIH

*At the banquet taking leave of Registrar Chang
at night*

The red candles are snuffed and brighten again;
The green flasks are refilled to the brim.
I care not that the road ahead is long;
Only I fear that this night may be too short.

CHU CH'ING-YÜ

Palace verse

Silent, silent in flower-time the courtyard door is
    closed;
Two fair ladies stand at the jade porch.
They make to talk of some palace affair,
But with the parrot before them they dare not speak.

23

TU CH'IU
(TU CH'IU-NIANG)

Gold thread coat

I ADJURE you, sir, not to prize your coat of gold
    thread;
I adjure you, sir, to prize the time of youth.
When the flower opens and is ready for plucking, it
    should straightway be plucked;
Do not delay until there is no flower, and pluck an
    empty twig.

TU MU

Parting, II

LOVE is here, but I can show no signs of love;
And before the wine-cups I feel that no smile will come.
Even the waxen candles have a heart to bewail this
    parting;
For us humans they drop tears until the dawn.

Returning home

MY small son tugs at my coat and asks;
'Why so late in coming back home?
With whom have you been racing the years and months
For this prize of silk-white hair?'

Travelling in the mountains

AFTER I climb the chill mountain's steep stone paths,
Deep in the white clouds there are homes of men.
I stop my carriage, and sit to admire the maple-grove at
nightfall,
Whose frozen leaves are redder than the flowers of early
Spring.

WÊN T'ING-YÜN

At the ferry south of Li-chou[1]

PLACIDLY the water's void breasts the slanting sun;
The crooked island, vast and boundless, merges into the
emerald hills.
Above the ripples a horse neighs, and the oars are seen
departing;
About the willows men wait for the ferry to return.
Amid clumps of sand-grass straggle flocks of gulls;
Over the boundless river-girt fields a single heron
flies.
But who so wise as to embark in search of Fan Li,[2]
Solitary in the mist and water of the Five Lakes,
forgetful of the World?

LI SHANG-YIN

Lo-yu yüan[3]

TOWARDS evening my soul was disquieted,
And I urged my carriage up to this ancient plateau.
The setting sun has boundless beauty;
Only the yellow dusk is so near.

Rising early

THE breeze and the dew make tranquil the clear dawn;
Behind the curtain there is one who alone is up betimes.
The orioles sing and the flowers smile –
Whose then, after all, is the Spring?

HSÜ HUN

Going up to the capital on an autumn day; inscribed on the tower of the T'ung-kuan post-station[1]

RED leaves rustle in the twilight;
In the long pavilion is one gourd of wine;
Fading clouds go home to the T'ai-hua mountain;[2]
Light rain passes the Chung-t'iao hills.[3]
The colours of the trees stretch from the frontier gate;
The sound of the river as it meets the sea is distant.
Tomorrow I will reach the Emperor's domain,
But I still dream of fishing and wood-cutting.

YEN YÜN

The fall of the flowers

THE splendour of Spring slowly, slowly departs – but
   whither?
Once more I face the flowers, and raise my cup.
All day I ask of the flowers, but the flowers make no reply:
For whom do you fade and fall?
For whom do you blossom?

CHAO KU

Thinking of the past in the tower by the river

In solitude I mount the riverside tower, sad at heart;
The moon shines like water, the water is like sky.
Where is she who came with me to admire the
  moonlight?
Yet the scene is not unlike a year ago.

SHÊN HSÜN

Drinking song

Shoot not the wild geese from the south;
Let them northward fly.
When you do shoot, shoot the pair of them,
So that the two may not be put asunder.

TS'UI LU

Parting at the end of spring

This rustic feast is disordered and without ceremony;
We speed you, sir, and speed also the Spring.
Next year when Spring's colours arrive,
See that you are not still away.

TS'AO SUNG

Written in the year Chi-hai (879), I

THE submerged country, river and hill, is a battle-
    ground.
How can the common people enjoy their wood-cutting
    and their fuel-gathering?
I charge thee, sir, not to talk of high honours;
A single general achieves fame on the rotting bones of
    ten thousand.

KUAN-HSIU

Inviting a friend to spend the night

SILVERED earth without dust, and the golden
    chrysanthemum in bloom,
Purple pears and red dates falling on the lichen moss;
A shaft of Autumn water, and a round moon –
On such a night, my old friend, are you not coming?

LO YIN

Bees

DOWN in the plain, and up on the mountain-top,
All nature's boundless glory is their prey.
But when they have sipped from a hundred flowers and
    made honey,
For whom is this toil, for whom this nectar?

CH'ÊN T'AO

« Lung-hsi song », II

THEY vowed to sweep away the barbarians without
  regard of self;
FIVE thousand in their furs and brocades perished in the
  Tartar dust.
Alas! their bones, lay beside the Wu-ting river;[1]
They still live in their ladies' dreams in Springtime.

YÜ FÊN

Facing the flowers

WHEN the flowers are in bloom, the butterflies cover
  the branches;
WHEN the flowers decay, the butterflies again are rare.
But there are the swallows in their old nest;
They return, however poor the master of the place.

SHAO YEH

« Bitter parting »

AT fifteen I plighted thee my troth;
At twenty I came into thy home.
Ever since I entered thy door,
I have seen thee prone to go away.
At morn I see friends speeding thee,
At eve I see friends speeding thee.
Were I told to snap each time a willow-whip,[2]

The trees here would not even have roots.
I would gladly be the earth on the roads,
And turn into dust on thy horse's hoofs.
I would gladly be a bent piece of wood,
And turn into two wheels for thy chariot.
But how can I get the T'ai-hang mountain,
And move it to block thy horse's way?

KAO CH'AN

Fisherman's life

THE untamed waters persist for a thousand years,
But the untended flowers become naught in a single
  night.
Nowadays the vain world has grown too narrow;
Can it compare with life in a fishing-boat?

LU KUEI-MÊNG

The wild geese

FROM South to North, how long is the way!
Between them lie ten thousand bows and arrows.
Who can say, through the mist and fog,
How many birds can reach Hêng-yang?[1]

WANG CHIA

After the shower

BEFORE it rained the first stamens were seen in the
flowers;
After the rain there is not a blossom at the leaves' base.
The butterflies stream over the wall,
In hope that Spring's colours may be found next door.

Ancient theme

YOU are on duty at the Hsiao Pass,[1] I am here in Wu;[2]
The west wind blows on me, and I am anxious for you.
For one line of this letter there are a thousand lines of
tears.
When winter reaches you, will your warm clothes have
reached you?

LÜ YEN

The cowherd

THE grass spreads across the common for six or seven
miles;
In the evening breeze he plays on his pipe three or four
notes.
Home again for a plenteous meal after the yellow dusk,
Without doffing his grass-coat he sleeps beneath the
moon's radiance.

TZŬ-LAN

On the city wall

THE ancient tombs lie thicker than grass;
The new graves encroach even on the highway.
Outside the city-wall there is no vacant ground;
Inside the city-wall men are still growing old.

CHÊNG KU

'Penny-moss'

RED in Spring, purple in Autumn, they encircle pond
  and terrace;
Each is round as a world-succouring coin.
After rain, to no purpose they fill the pauper lane;
They can buy me no flowers, only they buy me sorrow.

CHANG PIN

Lament for ten thousand men's graves

THE war is ended on the Huai border, and the trading
  roads are open again;
Stray crows come and go cawing in the wintry sky.
Alas for the white bones heaped together in desolate
  graves;
All had sought military honours for their leader.

KU HSIUNG

To « Declaring my inner feelings »

ALL night long you have deserted me; whither gone?
No news has come;
My scented chamber is closed.
Brows knitted, moon just setting,
How can I bear not to grope for you,
Weeping under my lonely coverlet?
Change your heart into my heart,
And learn the depth of my pining.

CHÊNG AO
(CHÊNG YÜN-SOU)

Riches and honour

A FAIR lady makes her toilet;
Her whole head is streaked with jewels.
How can she guess that two cloud-like tresses
Carry the tribute from many villages?

HAN HSI-TSAI

Feelings, I

*(Written on the wall of an official residence in the
central plain while on an embassy)*

NORTH of the River is my own land,
Now I am a settler South of the River.

Back I have come North on a visit;
But I lift my eyes and see no acquaintances.
The Autumn wind blows chill on me,
The Autumn moon is white – for whom?
Better that I return from whence I came,
For South of the River there are some who will care.

FÊNG YEN-CHI

To « The long-lived woman »

A SPRING day's feast,
One cup of green wine, one catch of song.
I bow again and utter three wishes:
First, I wish my good man long life;
Second, I wish for myself ever good health;
Third, I wish that we be like the swallows in the rafters,
Yearly meeting without a break.

LI CHIEN-HSÜN

Palace verse

THE palace door has long been shut – my dancing
   clothes are idle.
For a while I knew my lord and king, but now my hair
   is grey.
In truth I envy the fallen flowers which Spring cannot
   restrain,
As they float down the palace moat, and reach the world
   of men.

34

The day of the Ch'ing-ming festival

THEY all have carried forth their wine and sought the
    fragrant places;
For me alone, behind closed doors, there is quiet repose.
Only there are the poplar blossoms that seem to want
    my company,
On the wind ever and anon visiting my bedside.

LI YÜ

To « The fisherman »
(Two poems)

SPRAYS of wave purpose to make a thousand layers of snow;
Peach and plum trees, wordless, make Spring's cluster.
A bottle of wine,
A rod and reel –
In all the world how few are so well off as I?

A PADDLE in Spring's breeze, a leaf-like boat,
A silken line, a slender hook,
Flower-filled islet,
Wine-filled flask –
In the myriad ripples I attain freedom.

[First period]

Grief for a loved one
To « Pounding silk floss »

THE deep hall is silent,
The little courtyard is deserted.
Off and on go the taps on the cold slabs; off and on
    goes the wind.

Unendurable is the night's length and a man's
    wakefulness,
As a few sounds in the moonlight pierce the screened
    casements.

[Second period]

Grief for a loved one
To « Crows cawing at night »

WORDLESS, alone I climb the Western Tower;
The moon is like a hook;
In the solitude the Wu-t'ung trees in the deep courtyard
    are locked by cool Autumn.

That which scissors cannot sever,
And, sorted out, is tangled again,
Is the sorrow of separation,
With a flavour all its own for the heart.

[Last period]

Thinking of the past
To « Wave-washed sands »

OUTSIDE the curtains the rain goes splash, splash;
Spring's mood languishes;
My silken coverlet suffices not for the chill of dawn.
In my dream I knew not I was in exile,
And for one moment I indulged in pleasure.

Alone at dusk I lean on the balcony;
Boundless are the rivers and mountains.
The time of parting is easy, the time of reunion is hard,
Flowing water, falling petals, all reach their homes.
Sky is above, but man has his place.

[Last period]

WANG YÜ-CH'ÊNG

Written at Ch'i-an commandery[1]

I REMEMBER on a time in the Western Capital looking
    at peonies;
If the colour was slightly lacking my heart felt thwarted.
But now in this town amid the desolate mountains,
Even the blossoming of the Drum-flowers[2] gives me
    delight.

FAN CHUNG-YEN

Fisher folk on the river

MEN who come and go on the river,
All enjoy the savour of perch.
Pray look at that leaf-like boat,
Now seen, now unseen, in the windy waves.

OU-YANG HSIU

*Assistant Hsieh planting flowers
at the Secluded Valley*

THE light and the deep, the red and the white, should
    be spaced apart;
The early and the late should likewise be planted in due order.
My desire is, throughout the four seasons, to bring wine
    along,
And to let not a single day pass without some flower
    opening.

To « *Fresh berries* »

LAST year at the Lantern Festival
The flower-market lights were bright as day;
When the moon mounted to the tops of the willows,
Two lovers kept their tryst after the yellow dusk.

This year at the Lantern Festival
The moon and the lights are the same as then;
Only I see not my lover of yesteryear,
And tears drench the sleeves of my blue gown.

To « *Fisherman's pride* »

AFTER the parting I know not if he is far or near.
What meets the eye is bleak and doleful.
Slowly he journeys, slowly he goes farther, slowly his
  letters grow fewer.
Broad are the waters, deep swim the fish, where can I
  ask for him?

In depth of night the wind and bamboos tap out the
  music of Autumn;
Myriad leaves give a thousand sounds – all are
  lamentation.
So I choose the solitary pillow in search of dreams,
But dreams come not, and the lamp is guttering out.

WANG AN-SHIH

Early summer

A STONE bridge, a thatched cottage, a crooked ford;
Swiftly, swiftly the water flows between its two banks.
A bright sun, a warm breeze, the breath of the wheat-
  fields;
This green shade and peaceful turf are better than the
  time of flowers.

Night duty

THE golden bowl's incense burns to ashes, the sound of
  the water-clock fades;
Snip, snip goes the light breeze with its gusts of chill.
Spring's hues tease me, and I cannot sleep,
While the moon moves the shadows of the flowers up
  the balustrade.

LIU YUNG

To « The tune Kan-chou with eight rhymes »

BEFORE me the dreary, dreary evening rain spatters
  river and sky,
Wholly washing the Autumn clean.
Slowly comes the frost, and the bleak wind presses;
The frontier-pass and the river are cold and desolate;
And the dying sun fronts the tower.
Here the red grows sere and the green fades;
Slowly, slowly the glory of Nature departs.
Only there is the Long River's water
Silently flowing eastward.

I dare not climb on high to gaze afar,
For fear that my village is out of sight,
And the longing for home too hard to quell.
I sigh to think of these years of wandering;
What tarries me here to lament my lagging?
Methinks my fair wife has long watched from her tiring-
    room,
Oft beguiled as she marks a homeward ship on the
    horizon.
Little knowing that I am here leaning on this balustrade.
At this moment what heaped-up sorrow!

SU SHIH

Enjoying the Peonies at the
Temple of Good Fortune

IN my old age I adorn myself with flowers, but blush
    not;
It is the flowers that should blush for decking an old
    man's head.
Half tipsy I fumble along home, and men must be
    laughing at me,
For along the road half the folk have hooked up their
    blinds.

The cherry-apple

THE East wind floats gently through the noble hall;
A sweet mist damps the air, the moon comes round the porch.
My only fear is that in the depth of night the flowers
    will go to sleep,
So aloft I burn a silver candle to light their red raiment.

The washing of the infant

MOST men, bringing up sons, wish for them intellect;
But I by my intellect have had a life-time of failure.
I would only desire that my child should be simple and
 dull,
That with no ill-fortune and no troubles he may attain
 to highest office.

To « Water song »

(*At the Mid-autumn festival in the year ping-ch'ên (1076) I
enjoyed myself by drinking until dawn and became very drunk.
I wrote this poem, thinking of T₃ǔ-yu*)[1]

'BRIGHT moon, when wast thou made?'
Holding my cup, I ask of the blue sky.
I know not in heaven's palaces
What year it is this night.
I long to ride the wind and return;
Yet fear that marble towers and jade houses,
So high, are over-cold.
I rise and dance and sport with limpid shades;
Better far to be among mankind.

Around the vermilion chamber,
Down in the silken windows,
She shines on the sleepless,
Surely with no ill-will.
Why then is the time of parting always at full moon?
Man has grief and joy, parting and reunion;
The moon has foul weather and fair, waxing and
 waning.

In this since ever there has been no perfection.
All I can wish is that we may have long life,
That a thousand miles apart we may share her beauty.

Expression of my feelings
To « Burning incense »

THE clear night is dustless;
The moon is like silver.
When the wine is poured, let it fill to the brim;
Vain honour, vain wealth
Should cease to afflict the soul.
Alas, for the 'gallop of light'
For the spark of flint,
For the dream of body!

Though my bosom holds the fine and the elegant,
When I open my mouth who will befriend me?
Better be gay, and enjoy to the full nature's gifts!
When can I return home,
And be a man of leisure,
With a lute,
A jar of wine,
A cloud-filled stream?

YEN CHI-TAO

To « *Partridge sky* »

My many-coloured sleeves cordially held up the jade-
goblet,
At the feast I feared not to flush my cheeks with wine;
I danced until the moon over the tower came down to
the willows,
I sang until the peach-blossom fan had exhausted its
breeze.

After our parting
I thought of reunion.
Oft-times my spirit was with him in dreams.
At this remnant of night I shine the silver lamp on him,
Still in fear that our reunion is only in a dream.

CHOU PANG-YEN

To « *Wounded feelings* »

At the branch tops the faithful breeze abates;
I see the evening crows in flight.
Once more it is twilight;
I close the door and catch the afterglow.

South of the River my man has gone on a road
unknown.
His letters come not;
Only sadness is his harbinger.
I dread to see the solitary lamp,
As frosty cold urges me to an early bed.

MO-CH'I YUNG
(MO-CH'I YA-YEN)

Rain
To « Enduring love »

THE rain drips and drips!
The hour strikes and strikes!
Outside the window the plantain, inside the window the
    lamp,
At such a time the feelings are unbounded.

Dreams hard to fashion!
Regrets hard to smooth out!
No wonder a sorrower mislikes to hear:
In the empty courtyard the dripping lasts till dawn.

CHU TUN-JU

To « The fortune-teller »

BY the ancient rill there is a single plum-tree
That refuses to be imprisoned in garden or park.
Far away in the mountain depth it fears not the cold,
As though at hide-and-seek with Spring.
My inmost thoughts, who can know them?
Ties of friendship are hard to make.
Alone in my romance, alone in my fragrance,
The moon comes to look for me.

LI CH'ING-CHAO
(LI I-AN)

To « Spring at Wu-ling »[1]

THE wind stops, earth is fragrant with fallen petals.
At the end of day I am weary to tend my hair;
Things remain, but he is not, and all is nothing.
I try to speak but the tears will flow.

I hear it said that at the Twin Brook the Spring is still
    fair,
And I, too, long to float in a light boat.
Only I fear that the 'locust boat' at the Twin Brook,
Cannot move with a freight
Of so much grief.

HSIANG KAO

To « Like a dream »

WHO are the companions sitting alone at the bright
    window?
I and my shadow – the two of us.
When the lamp-light dies out and it is time to sleep,
Even my shadow deserts and hides away from me.
Alas! alas!
So sad and troubled am I!

LIN SHAO-CHAN

Journey at dawn
To « Eyes' fascination »

A GLOW ushers in dawn while the moon is still bright;
Over the sparse trees hang some fading stars.
On the hill-paths men are few;
In the depth of the blue wistaria,
Singing birds make two or three notes.

Petals of frost, heavy on my fur coat, strike chill,
But my heart is light as my horse's hoofs.
Ten miles of green mountain,
One stream of flowing water –
All add to the inspiration.

YANG WAN-LI

On the day of Cold Food, taking my sons to visit
the Ti garden and achieving ten poems

THE children will tire of running? – let them to the full!
My old legs ache a little, and I half wish for help.
I cannot know if the flowers ahead are good or not,
So I bid the bees and the butterflies to be my outriders.

Meditating in the pavilion by the poo

(Two Poems)

I

WEARY of sitting on the Tartar couch,
I arise and lean upon the trellis;
Now, while other men are busy, I am idle.
Even in idleness there is room for being busy:
The conning of books once ended, I con the hills.

2

BESIDE the water-lilies I play with the water until all
my body is scented;
Behind the bamboos I cool the air with a full fan.
Men say that when Autumn comes the days grow short
again,
But here is Autumn, and still the idler's day seems
longer than ever.

Again in praise of myself

THE river breeze urged me to sing;
The mountain moon bade me to drink.
In a stupor I fell down before the flowers,
With the sky and the earth as my coverlet and my
pillow.

LÜ PÊN-CHUNG

To « Picking mulberries »

I GRIEVE that my love is not like the moon over the
riverside tower:
South and North, East and West,
South and North, East and West,
Only constant companionship and no separation.

I grieve that my love is all too like the moon over the
riverside tower:
A brief waxing, and then a waning,
A brief waxing, and then a waning,
I wait for the full circle of union – but how short-lived!

LU YU

Kept indoors by the rain

THE East wind blows the rain along and vexes the
    rambler,
Filling the roads with fresh mud for their delicate dust.
The flowers sleep, the willows nod, Spring itself is idle.
Who could guess that I should be more idle than
    Spring?

FAN CH'ÊNG-TA

To « Eyes' fascination »

MELLOW, mellow at the sun's foot floats the purple
    mist;
The genial warmth dismisses my light fur.
Tired by the breath of heaven,
Drunk with the breath of flowers,
I dream at noontide with head on hands.

This lazy Spring is like the water of a pond in
    Springtime –
Wrinkled as by sorrow like a strip of crape.
Gently, gently, dragging and dragging,
The East Wind, strengthless,
Tries to make a ripple, but gives up.

HSIN CH'I-CHI

To « The ugly slave »

IN youth, not knowing the taste of sorrow,
I loved to ascend the storeyed towers,
I loved to ascend the storeyed towers,
And, to fashion new verses, I made myself speak of
   sorrow.

But now, having known all the taste of sorrow,
I should speak of it but refrain,
I should speak of it but refrain,
Instead, I say: 'A cool day, a fine Autumn'.

CHU SHU-CHÊN

Feelings on an autumn night, IV

VANQUISHER of the West Wind, tyrant of all
   blossoms,
The whole of Autumn's colours are busy in its behoof;
One plain twig is set beneath my study window –
Man and flower have in their hearts their own
   sweetness.

CHIAO-JU-HUI

Farewell to spring
To « The fortune-teller »

I HAVE a mind to speed Spring's departure
For I have no way to keep Spring here.
When all is said, year after year it has its uses;
Better that it does not go.

The eye stops short at Ch'u's far horizon;
It sees not the homeward road of Spring.
On the urgent wind even the peach-blossoms seem sad:
Speck by speck, flying like red rain.

TAI FU-KU

Seeing the pleasures of living in the mountains

A BROOK with twist and turn reaches the door-step,
On all sides are green hills that no picture can equal.
Tall bamboos shade the door, and plum-trees line the
    path.
Here is the place alike for a poet to dwell, and for a
    villager to dwell.

In a Huai village after the fighting

THE little peach-trees, ownerless, blossom untended;
Above the waste of misty grass the ravens home for the
    night.
Here and there broken walls encircle ancient wells;
Erstwhile, each of these was a man's habitation.

CHANG LIANG-CH'ÊN

Chance verses

WHOSE are this pond and house?
I lean on the red door, yet dare not knock.
But a fragment of sweet Spring cannot be hidden,
As over the coloured wall there peeps the tip of an
    apricot branch.

YEH SHAO-WÊNG

On visiting a garden when its master is absent

It is proper to hate the marks of shoes on the green
    moss;
Of ten that knock at this brushwood gate, nine cannot
    have it opened.
Spring's colours fill the garden but cannot all be contained,
For one spray of red almond-blossom peeps out from
    the wall.

KAO KUAN-KUO

To « The fortune-teller »

With much crooking of the fingers I counted for
    Spring's coming;
A snap of the fingers, and lo! Spring departs.
Out on the eaves the gossamer entangles the fallen
    petals,
Wishing likewise to keep Spring here.
How many days did I exult in Spring's sunshine?
How many nights did I lament Spring's rain?
The twelve carven casements and the six folds of the
    screen
Are all indited with verses that mourn for Spring.

LIU K'O-CHUANG

To « The fortune-teller »

EVERY petal is light as the butterfly's raiment;
Every speck is blood-red and tiny.
If you say that God cares not for the flowers,
Consider the hundred kinds and the thousand varieties,
  skilfully fashioned.

At morn you see the tree-tops luxuriant,
At eve you see the branch-tops denuded.
If you say that God, in truth, cares for the flowers,
Consider the rain's drenching, and the wind's blast.

YÜAN HAO-WÊN

Miscellaneous poems of mountain life, IV

BY the distant rill the maple-grove looks scattered;
By the deep mountain the lane of bamboos looks peace-
  ful;
The thin mist swallows up the departing birds;
The gleam of the sinking sun companions the homing
  kine.

CH'ÊN SHAN-MIN

Grass

THE grass may wither, but its roots die not,
And when Spring comes it renews its full life
Only grief, so long as its roots remain,
Even without Spring, is of itself reborn.

AUTHOR UNKNOWN

Parting
To « Partridge sky »

ALL the day I have had no heart to tend my dark
  eyebrows;
As the parting approaches I sorrow to see his travelling
  clothes prepared.
Before the flagon I fear only to hurt my good man's
  heart;
I restrain my tears that well up, and dare not let them
  drop.

I stay his noble steed;
I hold up the precious goblet.
We pour to each other, and exhort each other; but how
  to endure this parting?
Better to drink until I am the first to be overcome,
Intent on knowing not when my good man departs.

KAO K'O-KUNG

Passing through Hsin-chou[1]

FOR two thousand miles the land is fair with hills and
   streams,
Uncounted cherry-apples fringe the high road.
The wind bears along the fallen petals to mingle with
   the passing horses;
Those Winds of Spring, how they surpass even the
   wayfarers in their bustle!

LIU YIN

To « Magnolia flowers »

BEFORE the flowers open I often look if they are yet
   open;
And when they begin to open I fear that wind and rain
   may come.
After the flowers have opened I care not for wind and
   rain;
I only care if you come not, to drink deep beneath the
   flowers.

This year make not plans for next year:
Tomorrow's affairs will not be those of today.
The wind of Spring, wishing to admonish us here,
Lets drop one red petal before our eyes.

CHAO MÊNG-FU

The eastern city

By this rustic tavern the peach-blossoms flaunt their red
    allurements;
At the path-end the willows hang their misty catkins.
Had I not gone to say farewell at the Eastern City,
I had passed Spring's glory and known it not.

CH'ÊN CHIEH

Wind of spring

You touch the willows, and make a new green;
You breathe on the peaches, and restore a pristine red;
But for my fading countenance and my greying hair
I dare not blame you, O East Wind.

HUANG KÊNG

The village by the river

As far as the eyes can reach, river and sky stretch into
    the distance;
A cold mist veils the sun as it slopes to the West.
The fulness of Autumn's colours that no man rules,
Is half in vassalage to the rushes, and half to the water-
    weeds.

55

CH'ÊN YU-TING

Farewell to General Chao

THE length and breadth of all within the seas he will
    traverse,
But no signs of grief at separation are on his face.
The thought of years of lonely wandering
Is as the wind of Autumn and the chill of his sword-
    blade.

AUTHOR UNKNOWN

The fisherman
To « Magpie bridge »

A ROD beneath breeze and moonlight;
A grass-coat beneath mist and rain;
My home is on the west of the anglers' stage.
To sell my fish I dread to go near to the City's gate;
Still less will I consent to enter the depths of the Red
    Dust.

When the tide comes in, I untie the mooring;
When the tide is level, I ply the oars;
When the tide drops, I return home with a song.
Folk in their error say that I am another Yen Kuang,[1]
But I say that I am just a nameless old fisherman.

AUTHOR UNKNOWN

Plum-blossom

EVERYWHERE I have sought Spring but found not
    Spring,
As my straw-sandals trod the cloud-capped hills.
Back again, I playfully finger and sniff the plum-
    blossom,
And there, at the branch-tip, is all the fullness of Spring!

LIU CHI
(LIU PO-WÊN)

« *Sorrow on the jade steps* »

BENEATH the lamps of the Ch'ang-mên Palace my
    tears
Fell and become moss on the jade steps;
Every year with the Spring rain's influence,
Once more it creeps up this wall of the Imperial Park.

To « *Eyes' fascination* »

LUSH is the misty grass to the west of the little tower;
Clouds are low, and the wild geese cry softly;
Two rows of wide-spaced willows,
One streak of fading sunlight,
A few specks of perching crows.

Vernal hills and green trees renew their Autumn
    verdure,

But he is at the Wu-ling Brook.
Loveless is the bright moon,
But loving is the dream that comes,
Together they enter my solitary chamber.

LIU CHI
(LIU MÊNG-HSI)

A soldier's words: a soldier's wife's words

SAID the soldier to his wife:
'Whether I shall die or live I know not;
But if thou wilt solace my soul in the Yellow Springs,
Only care for our son in his swaddling clothes.'

Said the soldier's wife to the soldier:
'Thy body must needs be given to thy country;
But if thou shalt become dust at the frontier-post,
Thy wife will be the tablet-stone a-top thy mound.'

T'ANG YIN

Song of a life

MAN'S life from of old has rarely reached seventy;
Take away the early childhood years and the late years
    of old age;
Between these a man's time is not long.
And even so there is heat and frost, trouble and
    vexation.
Once past Mid-autumn the moon is less bright;
Once past April the flowers are less beautiful.

In the presence of flowers and beneath the moon if there
   is glad song,
In haste we should fill the golden goblet and pour it
   out.
On earth riches abound, but we cannot gain them all;
At the Court high ranks abound, but we cannot attain
   them all.
High rank and great riches only increase the heart's
   anxiety
So that our heads grow white too soon.
Spring, Summer, Autumn, Winter are as the twist of a
   finger;
The bell brings in the yellow gloaming, and then the
   cock announces the dawn.
I beg you, sir, to mark closely the men before your
   eyes;
Each year has its portion laid beneath the wild grass.
Beneath the grass how many are the tombs, high and
   low?
Each year has its half that no one tends.

YANG CHI-SHÊNG

*(Said to have been composed
on the way to execution)*

THIS infinite spirit I restore to the mighty void,
But a loyal heart will shine for whatever time.
All that in this life I have left undone
I bequeath to posterity to make good.

LI P'AN-LUNG

To « Enduring love »

Autumn's wind is pure,
Autumn's moon is bright,
Leaf on leaf the Wu-t'ung tree rustles outside the
    balcony;
Hard it is to build the dream of home.

On the steps the crickets chirp,
On the trees the birds flutter,
The frontier wild-geese, line upon line, breast the
    horizon,
Set upon wounding the exile's heart.

KUEI TZŬ-MOU

Face to face

In silence I sat facing my guest;
To the end I sat and said not a word.
I desired to make a show of friendship:
I sought in my mind but found nothing.
If good words are not joined to affection,
I trow that you, sir, would not desire such.
Our minds were open, and we both forgot each other;
What harm in this where you and I are concerned?

HUANG YU-TSAO

Chance verse on a summer day

In the deep hall the dust dissipates, the noon-tide heat
fades;
Smoke curls like a dream, and the day is lagging,
lagging.
The light wind seems in treaty with the lotus:
Bearing the fragrance along, it rolls up the curtain.

HSÜ T'UNG

To my younger brother

The Spring Wind should speed the traveller but,
instead, it grieves me;
On a strange road I meet Spring but deem it not to be
Spring.
I send forth words to the orioles that their songs should
not grow weary,
For beyond the horizon there is yet one who has not
returned home.

CH'I CHING-YÜN

*To the Licentiate Fu Ch'un on his
banishment to the frontier*[1]

One mouthful of Spring wine, and our love is ten
thousand miles apart.
Heart-breaking are the fragrant plants, heart-breaking
are the orioles.

Would that these two streams of tears might turn into
  rain,
To keep you, my love, from leaving the city tomorrow.

SHIH JUN-CHANG

*In farewell to Li Wan-an on his leaving office
and returning home*

AT this year's end the boat departs, light as a leaf;
Songs die down, wine stops flowing, and we both shed
  tears.
The sound of the shoal is not without compassion,
For its sobs follow and escort you on your way.

LIANG CH'ING-PIAO

*Spring day
To « Eyes' fascination »*

THE sun's rays shoot through the shining window;
  there is peace and not a sound.
In the light breeze the willow-branches bend.
There is one in the seclusion of her chamber,
In all her finery sitting alone,
With the door closed against the peach-blossoms.

Her memory is of bygone days as she turns her mind
  back;
Her heart's secret has been given to the cawing rooks.
Beyond the wall there is laughter and chatter.
Can it be that Spring's colours are only for her
  neighbour?

WANG YEN-HUNG

Brief partings, III

A CLUTCH at his war-coat, and our tear-stained cheeks
    touch:
The sails must needs be set for the urgent evening
    breeze.
Who says 'For a brief parting grieve not?'
This poor life of mine, how many brief partings can it
    endure?

HSÜ TSUAN-TSÊNG

The seventh night of the seventh month
To « Magpie bridge »

(*Yearly on this night the Spinning Girl is thought to cross the
Milky Way on a bridge of magpies to join her lover the Cow-
herd*)

SPARSE clouds and a faint moon –
Where can the bridge be built?
Surely the magpies are plentiful and the crows few.
Among mortals there is the nightly sharing of net-
    curtains,
But, alas! how easily does wedded bliss grow old.

For a whole year there is the grief of separation,
But now in early Autumn there is the glad reunion.
All through this night the two stars dread dawn's
    coming,
And I question: Had they not been severed by the
    Milky Way,
How could they feel the full joy of their meeting?

63

CHÊNG-YEN

On the lake
To « Rouged lips »

I come and go amidst the mists and waves;
In this life I call myself 'Master of the West Lake'.
With a light wind and a small oar
I paddle out from the rushy creek.

In high spirit I raise my song,
And in the quiet of the night my voice is wondrous
    clear.
But there is no one to enjoy it,
So I myself applaud,
As the song echoes from a thousand hills.

WANG SHIH-CHÊN

Crossing the Yangste in a gale, II

A pair of red-lapelled swallows lightly raid the wave-
    tops;
From either shore the petals fly as the breakers make a
    murmur.
Boats bound South and North pass, but cannot hail each
    other,
As with full sails they flash by, cleaving the river's water.

HSIAO-CH'ING
(FÊNG YÜAN-YÜAN)

Poems without title

I

I bow my head before the Goddess of Mercy:
May I not be reborn in the Western Land;
May I not be reborn in Heaven!
My prayer is to become a drop of water on thy willow-
branch,
Whose sprinkling may produce among mankind the
twin-stemmed lotus.

III

Bedecked anew I dare to vie with a painted picture;
I know not what would my rank be in the palace of the
Empress.
Ah, wasted form, reflected alone in the water of
Springtime,
Thou shouldst have the pity for me that I have for thee!

V

The cold rain on the gloomy window I cannot bear to
hear;
I turn up the lamp, and quietly read the 'Peony
Arbour'.[1]
The world has others as love-sick as I am,
Is it Hsiao-ch'ing alone that has a wounded heart?

WANG CHI-WU

Hsü Yu's gourd[1]

THE gourd hangs on the tree,
Light as a single leaf;
The wind blows it click-clack in the night.
It were best to cast it away that my dreams may be pure.
The whole world is not so great, the gourd is not so
small;
All things beyond the body are an encumbrance.

HSÜ LAN

Crossing the frontier

NESTLING on a mountain, looking down on the sea, is
the old frontier town;
Shadows of banners fluttering in the breeze show the
border keep.
Behind my horse are peach-trees in bloom, before my
horse is the snow;
As I pass the border, how can I forbear from turning
back my head?

WAN PANG-JUNG

Random thoughts

IF the world held no fame and no rank,
Men's hearts would all be as at the beginning of time.
If the world had no wheels and no hoofs,
Men would all keep to their native soil.
The Maker has chiselled order out of chaos,
Driving mankind plunging into nets and toils.
Who can fly beyond the heavens,
Far away like the yellow wild-swan's soaring?

YÜAN MEI

Miscellaneous poems, III

HEAVEN and Earth have their Spring and Autumn
Which come and go without end.
They lengthen not for the foolish,
They shorten not for the wise.
The wise know the value of pleasure,
And pleasure should be taken betimes.
What though I am to hunger tomorrow,
I am satisfied today.
What though I am to die next year,
I am living well this year.
If I cannot do what my heart desires,
A whitened head would still be as youthful death;
If I can rejoice for a moment,
Death at an early age would still be as a long life.

(1750/51)

To Yü-mên[1]

FROM South of the River to North of the River is a far,
    far way,
But before our doors it is the same stretch of water.
On the same day it can reach both of our homes;
Why are men unlike the tide of Spring?

(1750/51)

Standing at night at the foot of the steps

HALF bright, half dim are the stars;
Three drops, two drops, falls the rain.
Now the Wu-t'ung tree knows of Autumn's coming,
And leaf to leaf whispers the news.

(1760/61)

Chopsticks

I LAUGH that you should be so busy to pick up morsels,
And put them into others' mouths.
With a lifetime spent amid the sour and the bitter,
Can you or not distinguish the flavours yourself?

(1765)

The tree-planter laughs at himself

AT seventy I am still planting trees,
But let not my neighbours mock my folly.
From the beginning there has indeed been death,
But it is well that we have no fore-knowledge.

(1785)

From Hangchow visiting Su-sung,
P'i-ling, and Ching-k'ou and staying the night
with friends on the way

SEVENTY-SEVEN, such an old fellow!
In three years I get one look at the West Lake rains;
Back I come, place after place, for a short visit,
Troubling family after family to cook me chicken and
   millet.
My friends, forbear to ask the date of my next coming,
For this is an uncertain thing not for my ordering;
I keep saying I will never return and then returning,
And it is shameful to keep cheating folk like this.

(1792)

Expression of feelings, VII

ONLY be willing to search for poetry, and there will be
   poetry:
My soul, a tiny speck, is my tutor.
Evening sun and fragrant grass are common things,
But, with understanding, they can become glorious
   verse.

(1791)

A chance walk

I CHANCE to walk beneath the western porch;
Secluded, a solitary orchid has blossomed.
Who can it be that gave such early tidings
That already the bees have come?

69

CHAO KUAN-HSIAO

Treading the snow

I STAMP the snow to seek for the wood-cutter of the
  hill,
But the wood-cutter of the hill has stamped the snow
  and departed.
All the way are the tracks of his grass-shoes,
As my search leads me into the depth of the pine-woods.

YEH PAO-SUNG

Hsiao-ch'a shan pavilion

THE chill snow is heaped against the sunlit window;
I burn my incense, and rejoice to comprehend the Way
  of Buddha.
Out in the bamboos a bluecap calls,
And the breeze sways a snow-covered twig.

CHAO I

On my pillow

WITH head on pillow, I made a verse, but, mistrusting
  my memory,
I donned my coat and rose to write it under the
  guttering lamp.
My simple wife chuckled, 'Why all this trouble?
Even the children at their lessons do not fuss like this!'

KUO LIN

Unceasing rain

For thirty days there have not been many fine
    mornings;
My close-fitting cotton coat still feels light.
Above the lake three hundred small peach-trees
Together sprinkle their tears on this day of tomb-
    worship.

KUNG TZŬ-CHÊN

Miscellaneous poems of the year Chi-hai, V

Like a mighty flood is my grief at parting as the sun
    declines;
My singing whip points east to the far horizon.
But fallen petals are not heartless matter:
Transmuted into Spring soil they will again nurture
    flowers.

HUANG TSUN-HSIEN

At anchor for the night

In a single line the homing wild geese cast desolate
    shadows;
Huddled in pairs the wild ducks are still asleep.
Men's talk is hushed, the awnings are stilled,
The sands shine faintly, and the bamboos are dim.

So near to my village my heart in its dreams grows
    more urgent;
My ear hates the sound of the water pattering at my
    pillow.
I haste to use the first dawn to start the oar;
I throw open the hatch as the slanting moon is still
    companioned by some fading stars.

(1885)

LIU TA-PAI

The flower girl

1

SPRING's chill is sharp;
The little girl is comely.
One call breaks the dawn of the town at Spring.
'Flowers very fine!
Prices very fair!
Spring's glory to sell as cheap as you will!'

The family at the East complains of short measure;
The family at the West complains of under-size;
Upstairs there is a mild chiding for lateness.
The wind of Spring harries,
The flowers' hearts are vexed.
Tomorrow they will grieve for their early withering.

2

SOUTH of the River the Spring is early
South of the River the flowers are fine.
The flower-seller's cry invades Spring's slumber.
'Apricot blooms red!

72

Pear blooms white!'
At the head of the street, at the end of the lane, cry after
cry.

The richly dressed want them!
The plainly dressed want them!
How much of Spring can money buy?
The buyers smile;
The seller frets;
But rosy cheeks will all alike age with Spring.

(1924)

HU SHIH

A trifle

I TOO have wished not to love
That I might escape love's agony,
But now after much appraisement,
I willingly accept love's agony.

(1919)

To « By the river »

SCREENED by the trees the sound of the brook is a soft
jingle;
To welcome us the birds sing in a chatter.
Together we have penetrated the quiet path along the
winding stream;
I for you collect berries,
You bedeck my hair with blossoms.

Anon we sit together on the water-brink,
With a tree to shade the haughty sun.

Deep in talk we reck naught of the evening rooks:
At this hour there are only you and I,
And what room is there for them?

(1915)

PING-HSIN

Love

To escape from thoughts of love,
I put on my fur-cloak,
And ran out from the lamp-lit silent house

On a tiny footpath
The bright moon peeps;
And the withered twigs on the snow-clad earth
Across and across, everywhere scrawl 'Love'.

Notes

p. 1. 1. Reading *hao*.

p. 4. 1. *Book of Songs*, song 64.

2. Ch'in Chia's wife. There are preserved in c. 32 of the seventh-century encyclopedia *I-wên lei-chü* four letters, two by Ch'in Chia and two by his wife, which were supposedly written at the same time as the poems. For its literary excellence and interest we give the second of Hsü Shu's letters here.

You have favoured me with a valued message, and have also bestowed on me divers gifts. The warmth of your kindly thoughts is beyond expectation.

The mirror is a work of art; the hairpin is of wondrous beauty; choice as are the perfumes, the plain lute is even more pleasing. You have given these rare articles to unworthy me – a sacrifice of what you value. But for deep affection, who would have done this?

When I looked into the mirror and took up the hairpin, my thoughts became confused. I tried to play on the lute and chant some ballads, but my heart stood still. You bade me use the perfumes to sweeten my person and the bright mirror to reflect my countenance. These words are used in error; they mistake my sentiments. Of yore there was the *Song** writer's moving 'flying thistle-down', and Pan Chieh-yü sang 'For whom should I adorn myself?'† So the lute will not be played till your return; the mirror will

* Song 63, stanza 2, reads

> Since you, my lord, went to the East,
> My hair is like flying thistle-down
> It is not that I cannot anoint or wash it,
> But for whom should I adorn myself?

† From Pan Chieh-yü's *Lament for myself* (preserved in her biography in *Han-shu*, 97). Pan Chieh-yü was a concubine (hence the Chieh-yü) of the Emperor Ch'êng (33–7 B.C.).

not be used till you are back; before I again see your
bright countenance the precious hairpin will not adorn me;
and ere I again wait on you, the perfumes will remain un-
opened.

p. 6.   1. T'ai-hang is the name of the long mountain chain which
divides the North China plain from the modern province
of Shansi, but here it probably only refers to a peak at the
southern end (South-east Shansi).

2. Probably south of modern Chin-ch'êng (South-east
Shansi).

p. 7.   1. Title of *Song* 156 which begins:

> We marched to the Eastern Mountains,
> We went away and did not return.

2. The second part of this poem beginning with the line
'Since you, Sir, went away' has probably had more imita-
tors than any other single poem in the Chinese language.

p. 9.   1. A.D. 398–445; author of the dynastic history *Hou-Han shu*.

p. 10. 1. See p. 7.

2. Emperor Kao of the Ch'i dynasty (reigned 479–82).

p. 12. 1. When Su fell from power in 720 he was sent to a provincial
post at I-chou (modern Ch'êng-tu, Szechwan).

p. 13. 1. See p. 7.

2. This poem is the first of a famous series of twenty (*Wang-
ch'uan collection*) which Wang Wei wrote about features of
his country estate Wang-ch'uan at Lan-t'ien, south-east of
the capital Ch'ang-an. This estate had formerly belonged
to Sung Chih-wên. Included with Wang's own poems in
this collection are twenty poems on the same topics by his
friend P'ei Ti.

3. The Sung commentator Yang Ch'i-hsien identified the
Peach-blossom Pool as being at Ching-hsien, Anhui, and
stated that the descendants of Wang Lun, who supplied Li
Po with wine when he stayed here, still treasured the poem.
However, another site near Su-sung in South-west Anhui
is also claimed to be the place where Li Po took leave of
Wang Lun.

p. 15. 1. In 756 during the rebellion of An Lu-shan the poet moved his family to Fu-chou, north-east from Ch'ang-an. When he left them to join the fleeing court, it must be presumed that he fell into the hands of the rebels and was taken to Ch'ang-an, where he wrote this poem.

p. 15. 2. Written in the spring of 761, when Tu was living at Ch'êng-tu, Szechwan.

p. 16. 1. Hua Ching-ting who in 761 suppressed a rebellion in the Szechwan area. Tu Fu, living in Ch'eng-tu ('the City of Brocade'), seems to have been friendly with him.

p. 18. 1. Li Shih-tao raised a revolt, and was executed in 819.

p. 19. 1. Imperial park at Ch'ang-an.
2. West of Ch'ang-an.

p. 20. 1. Ancient chronicles were scratched on green bamboo slabs.
2. Name of hills near Lo-yang used as a cemetery.
3. The favourite disciple of Confucius (514–483 B.C.).
4. One of two famous brothers who preferred starvation to disloyalty (eleventh century B.C.).

p. 22. 1. Conventional figure for a life span.
2. Têng Yu saved his brother's son and abandoned his own while fleeing to the south after the fall of North China to the Huns in 316. His wife did not bear him another son but he refused to take a concubine. Thus he died without an heir.

p. 23. 1. P'an Yüeh (247–300) wrote three poems in mourning for his wife (*Wên-hsüan*, c. 23).

p. 25. 1. Modern Kuang-yüan, Szechwan.
2. A famous statesman of the fifth century B.C., who at the height of his power disappeared from the Five Lakes.
3. On the south-east edge of the capital Ch'ang-an. It was the highest point in the city area and thus a place of resort at the spring and autumn festivals.

p. 26. 1. T'ung-kuan is the pass which leads to the T'ang capital Ch'ang-an (modern Si-an) from the east.
2. The western sacred mountain south-west of the T'ung-kuan pass.
3. The Chung-t'iao range extends in a north-easterly direction from the T'ung-kuan pass.

p. 29. 1. The Sangkan which flows out of Suiyuan to join the Yellow River in Shensi.

2. In Chinese literature a willow-branch given to a departing one is an emblem of godspeed.

p. 30. 1. The main peak of the seventy-two peaks of the Hêng-shan group, which lies south of the town of Hêng-yang, Hunan; it is traditionally the southern limit of the migration of the wild geese whence they return in the spring. Hence it is also called the Turning Geese Peak.

p. 31. 1. In modern province of Kansu, leading into Central Asia.

2. Probably used loosely for South China.

p. 37. 1. Modern Huang-kang, Hupei.

2. Bindweed.

p. 41. 1. His younger brother, Su Chê.

p. 45. 1. Believed to have been written after the death of the author's husband.

p. 54. 1. North-west of modern Shang-jao, Kiangsi.

p. 56. 1. A fellow-student of the first Emperor of the Later Han dynasty, Kuang-wu (reigned A.D. 25–57). On Kuang-wu's accession, Yen Kuang changed his name and became a recluse, steadfastly refusing the Emperor's offers of appointment.

p. 61. 1. The story attached to this poem is that Ch'i Ching-yün, a very cultivated singing-girl, fell in love with Fu Ch'un and when he was charged with a crime and imprisoned, she sold her ornaments to provide for him. When he was banished to the frontier, she wished to accompany him but was not permitted. She then shut herself up and soon after fell ill and died.

p. 65. 1. The most famous of the operas of T'ang Hsien-tsu (1550 – 1616).

p. 66. 1. Hsü Yü – a notable minister of the mythical ages, who turned hermit. The gourd water-dipper was provided by a friend to save him from using his hollowed hand, but even when it was hung out of use its sound was felt by him to be too sensual.

p. 68. 1. Ch'êng Chin-fang (1718–84), well known as a bibliophile.

Index of Poets

INDEX OF POETS